PLAN B

ST. CLAIR FAMILY SERIES

BOOK ONE

ERIN STEVENSON

Happy Jack Publishing

Copyright © August 2018
by Erin Stevenson Quint

Cover Design by Tina Lampe

DEDICATION

To Mom, who taught me to always have a Plan B.

ACKNOWLEDGMENTS

I am so grateful for my 5K critique group and other writers in the Des Moines Writers' Workshop. You have lifted me up and made me a better writer. I hope that I have done the same for you.

Many thanks to Beth Burgmeyer of Happy Jack Publishing Company, most of all for your friendship, and for helping to make this dream come true.

Finally, to my children for your support—once you got over the shock of finding out that your mother was writing books!

1

"SO, KELSEA DENISE, what's your Plan B?"

I rolled my eyes and grabbed another tissue.

"And don't roll your eyes."

My head flopped back on the pillow. How could my mother know I was rolling my eyes, over the phone, from two hundred miles away? I rolled them again to see if they made any noise. No sound whatsoever.

"I'm working on it, Mom, I'll be fine."

"You have to have a Plan B, sweetheart. You can't just pick up and move on without a plan." I tuned her out. I had heard this more times in my almost three decades than I could count. My brain rejoined the conversation a few moments later.

"...and if I hadn't had my teaching degree to fall back on, you and Morgan and I would have starved when your father died," Mom said softly.

I stopped my eyes just as they began to roll. Dad had been well insured, but I knew it gave Mom a sense of purpose to have gone back to teaching.

"I know, Mom, but Ryan didn't die." *However, that could be arranged.*

"Breaking your engagement four days before the wedding! I never would have believed it from that boy. He was so nice."

"Yeah, I know, Mom. He had everyone fooled." *Most of all, me.*

A maternal sigh rippled through the miles into my ear. "And *so* handsome! Both of you with that gorgeous dark hair and brown eyes. You would have given me beautiful grandchildren."

Would you like some cheese with your whine, Mom?

My mother was desperate for a grandchild, and that task rested completely on my slim shoulders. All of her close friends had about seventy-five grandchildren apiece. My sister, Morgan, was off the hook. She'd breezed through college, motored through a master's and Ph.D., and was now Assistant Professor of Art Therapy at the Midwest Art Institute in Chicago. She wasn't even thirty yet. Morgan was too busy with her teaching and her patients and her research to think about dating or marriage or children, but because of her sparkling success, Mom never harassed *her.*

Time to shut this down. I tossed the crumpled tissue into the overflowing wastebasket and rose up from my messy day bed, where I'd spent the last day and a half sobbing my soul out. I walked through the living room into the kitchen (which took a full five seconds), grabbed the plastic container from the bottom shelf of the pantry, and shook dog food into a bowl.

If masked men with automatic weapons burst into my tiny apartment to abduct me, my dogs would sleep through it and never see or think about me again. But the tinkling sound of their food landing in the ceramic bowl was all that was needed for the barkfest to commence.

"Mom, I've got to let the dogs out," I yelled over the din. "I'll talk to you later."

"All right, Kelsea, remember your Plan B. I'll check in with you tomorrow. Love you."

Oh, joy. "Love you, too, Mom." I hit *end* and tossed my phone down on the counter.

I *did* love my mom, but I was nothing like her. Morgan was like her. Morgan always had a Plan A, B, C, and D. If, on the other hand, flying by the seat of one's pants was an Olympic sport, I would win the gold medal.

I shuffled to the fridge and pulled out the milk. According to the date stamp, it would expire today. *How does the milk know to just give up on the 29th?* I decided to take my chances. It wasn't like *Ryan* or anyone would know or care if I died from milk poisoning or whatever happens when you drink expired milk.

I grabbed the Oreos and sat down at my small table. Penny and Sheldon were still scarfing down their food. The two Poms came into my life about four years ago when I first started volunteering at the animal shelter. They were the best thing to ever happen to me.

I looked at the clock and decided that this was dinner. After polishing off a few—all right—a lot of Oreos (and the milk, which tasted fine), I wiped my hands on a napkin and opened my laptop. I had ignored all the notifications and messages of shock and awe about the canceled wedding. I had no desire to talk with anyone about it. Thank God we had kept things relatively small and local, despite Ryan's mother's attempts to make this the social event of the season.

Morgan was my only attendant, and Ryan's best friend was his best man. It should have been easy enough to cancel the church, photographer, flowers, cake, and the restaurant where we were going to have the reception. Since Ryan's mother arranged all of it, I suppose she canceled all of it.

A new message popped up in my e-mail. *Flight itinerary for Ryan Patrick Singer and Kelsea Denise Anderson.*

I groaned out loud. The honeymoon! How could I have forgotten? The tears began to flow again, and I reached into my pocket for a rumpled tissue.

It was the only aspect of the entire event in which I had any say. The moment we announced our engagement, Jasmine Singer morphed into the monster-in-law-slash-wedding-planner-from-Hades.

She even chose the wedding date. New Year's Day.

I finally convinced Ryan to let me arrange the honeymoon and pay for it. And keep it a complete surprise from everyone, including him.

I blew my nose with a loud honk. In exactly three days, I would have been with the love of my life on a plane to a Caribbean island for a week at a romantic honeymoon resort. Just the two of us and approximately one hundred other bridal couples. No single lotharios, no families with noisy children, no old people.

I took one more drink of milk and, just to punish myself, clicked on the link for the resort at the top of my *Favorites*. I already had the pictures memorized. All that sand and surf and romance! I stamped my feet and let out an angry squeal. Sheldon and Penny looked up at me, and Penny padded over. "Come here, baby," I cooed, picking her up.

4

Her large, innocent eyes stared at me, and she rubbed her head under my chin as I hugged her close. Penny always knew when I needed comforting.

Tears blurred my vision as I looked at the screen again. *Wait a minute*...I perked up and started clicking. *What if...?*

I already knew that there were absolutely no refunds in the event of a cancellation. That had been spelled out loud and clear in several places throughout the resort's website. After a thorough search, I made up my mind. There was nothing whatsoever that stated that I couldn't still go there *alone.* I had scrimped and saved for it, and painstakingly rearranged my schedule and gotten coverage to be gone for the week. A shiver rippled through me. Most of all, I had looked forward to a break from the St. Louis winter.

Who would care? All those couples would be staring into one another's eyes. No one would even notice me. I could still read and take walks and swim and soak up the sun. *I deserve this.*

I kissed Penny and held her up in front of me. "That's it, girl, I'm doing this! I'm going on a honeymoon!"

Her reply was an enthusiastic yip.

I stared out the window as the jet began its descent into St. Jardin International Airport. I was completely mesmerized by the blue and turquoise waters, the sun sparkling on it like diamonds. In the distance, on the island itself, I could see foliage in myriad shades of green. The effect was incredibly soothing. "Nice job, God," I whispered. Then I began to think about what it must have been like during Creation week. Did He get everything right on the first try? Probably, because

He's—well, God. But what if even He didn't get it right every time, and occasionally had to come up with a Plan B? What if He realized that the giraffe's neck was too long, and instead of shortening it, decided to add some taller trees?

I collected my luggage and climbed aboard the first of two shuttle buses that were waiting just outside the terminal, as promised. Even if I hadn't been directed where to go, the two-tone pink bus with the sprawling words "St. Jardin Honeymoon Resort" in silver script would have been the first clue.

"Kelsea, um, Anderson," I said in a low voice to the petite, young woman with the clipboard standing at the top of the steps. She was dressed from head to toe in the same colors as the bus, and her bright pink nametag read *Molli*, with an *i*. How appropriate.

"Anderson, Anderson," she murmured, a frown creasing her brow.

"It might be under *Singer*," I whispered. "But Ryan Singer isn't coming."

Her head snapped up, and her blue eyes popped wide open. "Isn't coming?"

"Correct," I replied. "I'm here alone. I paid for our reservation."

"This is highly unusual," Molli stated. Her blond ponytail danced as her head shook back and forth. "We've been open for almost three years, and we've never had—"

I interrupted her, trying to sound authoritative without being mean. "It may be unusual, but your website didn't say a thing about not being able to come alone. I've paid for the week." I kept my gaze even and steady.

"Well, all right, Mrs.—Miss Anderson." She pointed to

the empty seat behind the driver. "Take a seat. You'll have to talk with the owners when we get to the resort."

"Thank you," I managed to croak as I pushed by her and slid into the seat. At least she didn't throw me off the bus.

I set my purse and carry-on next to me, turned my head toward the window, and swallowed the lump in my throat. *Breathe, Kelsea, you can do this.* Once I got to the resort and into my room, I could hide in there, order room service, and figure out ways to keep to myself, especially to avoid the advertised "newlywed games" and other social mixers.

The palm trees swayed in the warm, tropical breeze as I stared out the window. Even if it was uncomfortable to be at the couples' resort alone, it was worth it to be away from the snow and ice at home. I could spend the week figuring out my Plan B. My mother would be so proud.

Happy, smiling couples boarded the bus two-by-two, just like Noah's Ark. I averted my gaze and tried to tune out their laughter as they began socializing with one another.

"Miss Anderson?" It was cute little Molli-with-an-i, all efficiency. "We have a situation. A couple of our entertainers missed their flight last night and just arrived, and we need every seat on both shuttles." Her gaze flicked to the items sitting on the seat next to me.

"Oh, okay," I mumbled, gathering my things onto my lap. I turned my attention back to the scenery outside the window.

A moment later, the seat shuddered as a weight landed on it. A solid arm pressed into my shoulder, then shifted away.

"Sorry," a deep male voice growled. He didn't sound sorry at all.

Gosh, this guy was big. Not fat, just—well, big.

Muscular with long legs that stuck out into the aisle. Still, his knees were nearly touching his chest. This shuttle bus wasn't made for someone his size, and he more than filled his half of the seat. I scooted closer to the window and snuck another look at him.

A blond Adonis. Not bad looking, if you liked the type, which I didn't. My type was TDH—tall, dark, and handsome. *Ryan.*

I opened my mouth to offer a sharp retort, then thought better of it. If this guy was one of the entertainers, he might be one of the few people at the resort that I could talk to or even hang out with a little, just to pass the time.

I pasted on a smile. "So, are you a singer, or dancer? Wait, let me guess. A magician?"

His amber eyes blazed. "Mind your own business, lady," he snapped, and turned away.

LANDON ST. CLAIR stared into the crystal clear liquid and lifted the glass to his lips. As soon as the liquor entered his mouth, he fought to swallow it, and sputtered. He rubbed a hand over his eyes. "Ach, what am I doing?" he muttered to himself, and set the glass down on the bar with a hard clink. He stood, took out his wallet, and tossed down some bills.

Landon had never been a big drinker, even in college. He enjoyed a couple of beers at a party or at a sports bar with friends. He never liked the taste of the hard stuff, and once he had experienced his first hangover, decided that it wasn't worth it.

Only being left at the altar would drive him to even consider crossing that line.

He left the resort bar and walked through the pink-themed lobby to the dining hall, but his mind was miles away. The image of standing in front of five hundred guests waiting for his bride to enter was burned into his memory. The music began to play, the six bridesmaids entered one by one, and then the doors closed. The members of the string ensemble held their instruments still, poised to launch into the bridal march. Silent seconds turned to minutes. The mother of the bride sat wild-eyed on the front row, her head swiveling between the bridal party in front and the door in back. Landon stared at the door, willing Nicola to enter.

And then he knew with certainty what he had felt in his gut for the last two days. That she wasn't going to go through with it. She wasn't going to marry him.

Now, almost exactly twenty-four hours later, Landon was alone on the Caribbean island of St. Jardin—the *Island of Gardens*. Well, *alone* as one could be with approximately two hundred honeymooners. He'd carefully checked all the legal disclaimers and decided to keep his reservation, hole up in his room, and figure out a Plan B.

Other than giving his name to the pink-clad girl on the shuttle bus, and snapping at his perky, nosy seatmate, he hadn't said a word to anyone until he'd arrived at the resort.

The check-in process had been uncomfortable, and when Landon announced that he was here alone and that *no, * Mrs. St. Clair would *not* be joining him, the owners were immediately summoned. Rosie and Ike Goldman clucked sympathetically and assured him that they would do everything in their power to make his stay tolerable if not enjoyable.

Landon squirmed in his tux as he waited to meet the Goldmans as instructed. He'd been loath to put it on again, but had little choice, since tonight's dinner was black tie. For once, he wished he was closer to average height. It was hard to fade into the woodwork when you were six foot four.

Everywhere he looked, there were couples entwined, or holding hands, or staring into each other's eyes, sending loaded messages. Landon fought the urge to bolt from the building. *What was I thinking? I wish hadn't come.*

I CHECKED MYSELF in the full-length mirror one more time. *Eat your heart out, Ryan.*

The emerald green chiffon dress certainly made a statement, along with the three-inch black platform peep toe heels that I'd snagged at a vintage shop for a fraction of their worth. I do love a good bargain.

My hair had even cooperated tonight. I'd fashioned it into a surprisingly elegant updo with the help of several small, glittering clips, and thanks to the humidity, tendrils framed my face in a way that looked both effortless and chic.

All the clothes I'd bought for the honeymoon were back home, the tags still on them. At least I could return them. The lingerie, however, had been offered up as a burnt offering to spinsterhood in my metal trashcan. So I landed on St. Jardin with a suitcase full of mostly sloppy, comfortable clothes. But I couldn't part with the green dress, and it wouldn't hurt to make a good first impression tonight. It would be all downhill from here.

I swiveled my hips, first one way and then the other, and

watched the skirt gently float out and then settle back just above my knees. "Not bad for a dog walker from Kirkwood, Missouri," I said to the glamorous woman in the mirror.

Small business owner, the voice in my head corrected me. I'd survived the first year, and my client list was growing. I was still astounded at the vast sums that people would shell out to have their dogs walked, played with, fed and watered, taken to the dog park, and even to the doggie day spa for pampering. Due to referrals from my happy dog owners, I was branching out to care for cats, birds, rabbits, and the occasional gerbil and ferret. I drew the line at reptiles.

I drew my black silk shawl around my shoulders, picked up my clutch and, out of habit, looked for my phone. I didn't have a very good plan, and now that I was flying solo, I couldn't afford to indulge in international minutes. Before I left for the airport, I sent a text to Morgan. *Leaving my phone at home. I just need to unplug. You have the contact info for the resort. Will you explain to Mom? I know, I owe you! Love you* ☺ Then I powered it down and left it on my kitchen table.

My stomach let out a growl, and even though I wasn't looking forward to having to socialize with people tonight, there was no other option. I wasn't happy during the check-in process when Molli informed me that there was no room service for meals.

"Can you imagine? If we allowed that, our staff could never deliver two hundred meals to a hundred rooms. No one would want to come out," Molli had lamented dramatically. "Dinner is at eight o'clock sharp. The first night is formal, and the owners will be there to meet everyone. They're busy right now, but they're particularly looking forward to meeting *you,* Ms. Anderson," she added with a lift of her right eyebrow. It looked mysterious and exotic.

I turned to the mirror and tried to lift one eyebrow, and then the other. It didn't look mysterious or exotic on me, it looked like I was having gastric issues. I guess independent eyebrow mobility is like having double joints, you either have it, or you don't.

It was a quick walk to the main lodge. I got in line in the lobby and stood there among—what else?—loving couples, and kept my head down. I had no desire to draw attention to myself. When I got to the check-in table, there was Molli—now decked out in a formal in the same shade of pink that she wore previously, that matched the bus and all the signage and decorations at the resort. There was another girl sitting next to her whose pink nametag read *Haley.* She wore a formal in a paler shade of pink.

I had a feeling I was going to see more pink over the next week than I'd seen in my entire life, although I had to concede that someone had done a fantastic job of making it all look very elegant.

"Name, please?" said Haley.

You have every right to be here. State it loud and proud. "Kelsea Anderson."

Molli had just finished with another couple and perked up when she heard my name. "Oh! This is the one I was telling you about," she said to Haley. "She's the one who *came here ALONE.*" Her voice rose in volume until she was practically shouting those last three words. *Say it a little louder, would you, Molli? They couldn't quite hear you back in St. Louis.*

14

Haley nodded solemnly. "Oh-h-h-h." She drew the syllable out for several seconds. "Rose wants to talk to you," she said, her eyes growing wide.

"Rose is the owner," Molli clarified. She stood. "Come with me."

My stomach churned. Was Rose the owner going to throw me out? My mind conjured up a dark, menacing creature pointing a long, crooked finger toward the door. *Off my island!* her evil, witchy voice roared. I trailed after Molli through the middle of the room, which was filled with round tables that seated eight. Romantic candlelight illuminated each table, and there were twinkly pink and white lights everywhere. *Where in the world does one find pink lights?*

Molli arrived at what looked to be the main table, front and center. "Here we are," she said. "Rose, this is the woman you wanted to meet. Kelsea Anderson, this is Rose Goldman."

Before me stood a tiny woman with white hair with pink highlights, swept up in a bouffant à la 1965, topped off by a glittering pink and white tiara. *Surely those aren't real diamonds! And what gemstone is pink? Topazes?* She wore pink rhinestone-encrusted cat glasses and a hot pink vintage satin formal that looked brand new. I thought I had seen everything until my gaze landed on her feet, which were encased in—wait for it—pink Converse!

It should have been a totally ridiculous look, but somehow, she pulled it off. She was just adorable.

The elfin woman followed my gaze, which remained fixed on her feet, and shrugged. "Bunions."

She couldn't have been more than five foot two, and that included the poufy hairdo. She was seventy if she was a day, but her smile lit up the room, and melted my heart. The evil witch vacated my head, and my knees nearly went weak with relief.

"Kelsea Anderson, I'm so happy you're here," she said sweetly, encasing my hand in both of her soft, wrinkled ones. "I'm Rose, but my friends call me Rosie, and I hope you will, too." With me in my platform heels, she had to tip her head way back to look up at me. I felt like she could see straight into my soul. She spent a long moment appraising me, then lowered her voice to a conspiratorial whisper and patted my hand. "I can tell you're one of the strong ones. Good for you for coming. You're going to be just fine."

I swallowed the lump in my throat as she shooed Molli away with a bejeweled hand. "Molli, dear, Kelsea will be just fine with me. You go on back to the lobby now." Her bracelets tinkled as her arm waved.

Two couples were already settled in at the main table, totally into one another and oblivious to everything around them. That left four empty chairs. I assumed three were for Rose, her husband, and me. As I eyed the remaining chair, a feeling of trepidation washed over me.

"Those are the Wilders and the McFaddens," Rose said, pausing briefly. I'll introduce you later. Come with me." She smiled and nodded at people as she dragged me behind her. "Oh, there's my Ike. Yoo hoo, Ike!" Her face lit up and she waved. "Here he comes with your dinner companion."

I stopped dead in my tracks. I needed a dinner companion like I needed a third eye. I could barely manage shadow, eyeliner, and mascara for the two I already had, not to mention the hassle of the accompanying eyebrows. "Oh, Rosie, no. I don't need—"

She tugged on my hand. "It will be fine, dear. Trust me."

This would *not* be fine. My stomach gave a painful spasm and I took a deep breath, sending up a prayer for patience. I would have stayed in my room and skipped dinner altogether, but I'd hardly eaten over the last four days, and suddenly found that I had an appetite, which had now vanished.

Rose stopped as a white-haired man with bright blue eyes approached us. My stomach dropped when I realized who was with him. My seatmate from the bus, Mr. Rude Seat Hog.

LANDON COULDN'T BELIEVE it when Ike Goldman turned to him with a bright smile and said, "Will you look at my lovely bride? Fifty-three years last June, and she's still as beautiful as the day I made her mine."

Landon almost blanched, not because of Rose Goldman's outrageous pink ensemble, but because of the woman that she was pulling along behind her.

He fought the urge to groan out loud. *Is that Miss Perky?* It was hard to tell. The woman on the bus looked small and miserable, hunched down in the seat. This woman stood proud and tall, though not as tall as Nicola. The green dress was the perfect complement for her upswept, dark brown hair, not to mention a welcome respite from all the pink surrounding them. She had a nice figure, and wasn't bad looking, if you liked the type, which he didn't. Landon had always preferred blondes or redheads.

Then her eyes flashed with recognition, and her full, shiny lips twisted as if she'd sucked on a lemon. Yes, this was definitely the woman from the bus. *Great.* Where was her husband, anyway? Probably hiding out in the bathroom, if he had any sense.

Rose beamed and looked up at her husband. It was a short distance, since he was only a few inches taller than her. "Ike, this is Kelsea Anderson. My husband, Ike Goldman."

Kelsea Anderson's features relaxed, and her face was transformed. "It's a pleasure to meet you, Ike," she said warmly, and reached for his wrinkled hand with her smooth, elegant one. *Wow.* She was almost pretty.

Rose took a breath and gestured toward Landon. "And this gentleman is Mr. St. –"

"St. Fair. Brandon St. Fair." Landon interrupted, hoping he didn't sound too forceful. He didn't offer his hand. This had been his one request when he met the Goldmans, that they permit him to use an assumed name for the duration of his stay at the resort. He didn't want anyone wondering why he was here alone and then googling his name. Landon was certain that the leading news story in St. Louis was that a partner of the city's most prestigious law firm had been left at the altar by the daughter of one of the top families on St. Louis' social register.

Rose smiled. "Yes—Mr. St. Fair. This is Miss Anderson."

Miss? Landon's eyes flicked to the woman's bare left hand. He saw the gleam in Rose's eye, and smelled a set-up coming. And by the look on the brunette's face, she smelled it, too.

"Miss Anderson finds herself in the same unfortunate predicament as yourself, Mr. St. Fair," Rose explained. "She is here alone. In the almost three years that Ike and I have owned this resort, we've never had anyone come here on their own, and now we have you two." She smiled brightly at them. "Obviously, a single person here upsets the balance, and we don't want any of our guests to feel uncomfortable. If the two of you would, say, sit together at meals, you'll just blend in with everyone else, and attract less attention."

"I really don't think—" Landon began.

"I'll be fine on my own—" Miss Anderson's words came out on top of his.

Rose smiled up at them. "I'm so glad that's settled," she said sweetly. "Let's find our seats." And before Landon knew what had hit him, Rose had placed Miss Anderson's hand in the crook of his elbow, and they were following the Goldmans through the dining room to the head table.

He glanced down at the woman. She looked like she'd just eaten a prune, and walked stiffly next to him, her hand positioned in such a way as to have as little contact with him as possible.

Landon smirked at her. "I don't have cooties, you know."

Her head snapped up. "What are you, like twelve?"

Landon pasted on a smile as they arrived at the table. *Let the games begin.*

5

COOTIES? HEY, THE seventies called, they want their word back. What a dweeb.

Staying in my room and starving would have been far preferable to this farce, although I had to admit, the food was delicious. So Mr. high-and-mighty Brandon St. Fair wasn't one of the entertainers. He was just a jilted groom, apparently. *No surprise there. That woman sure dodged a bullet.*

"How long have you two been together?" This question came from the chatty Mrs. McFadden.

The dweeb looked at me, and his gaze softened just a bit. "Oh, it seems like minutes, really. Time just flies when you're having fun." He took a sip of his water.

My heart skipped a beat. His eyes were the dreamiest shade of amber I had ever seen, like fine cognac. *Wait, how would I know that? I've never had cognac.*

"Where are you from?" Julie McFadden chirped.

I wasn't about to let him answer all the questions directed to us. "Kirkwood, Missouri. A suburb of St. Louis," I quickly replied.

A shadow crossed Brandon's face. "Ike, could you pass the rolls, please?" he asked. "These are the best rolls I've ever had."

The bread basket made its way over to us. "We have a wonderful baker, as well as a top-notch chef," Ike said proudly.

Brandon held the roll basket out to me. His eyes held a threat of challenge. "You want one, pumpkin?" *Those eyes.*

"I'm fine, honey bunny," I replied, adding an adolescent giggle for fun. His eyes narrowed slightly and darkened a shade. *Ooh, this could be fun.*

He gave me an ingratiating smile. "You're so disciplined, sugar plum," he said as he slapped about a cup of butter on his roll. "You know how those carbs go straight to your hips."

The utter nerve of this man! I suddenly had the urge to smear the front of his tux with butter.

Mr. McFadden and Mr. Wilder both suppressed a laugh. Brandon smiled and winked at me. "Just kidding, sweet cheeks."

I'll show you my sweet cheeks, buster! No, I couldn't do that to Rose and Ike.

Mr. McFadden turned to the Goldmans. "You say you've owned this resort for three years? How did that come about?" I was happy that the conversation was no longer on my hips.

Rose and Ike shared a loving look and laughed. "Oh, we won the lottery!" Rose exclaimed.

"We played the same numbers every week for over twenty years, and finally hit the jackpot." Her big blue eyes, magnified by her cat-glasses lenses, darted around the table. I could tell that she couldn't wait to answer the question on everyone's minds. "Fifteen million!" she announced. We all responded with happy amazement.

Ike picked up the story. "Up until that time, we'd hardly been out of Brooklyn. But we sold our apartment and headed for the Caribbean. Never looked back. We threw a dart at a map, ended up on this island, and this resort was for sale. We had no idea what we were going to do with it, but we bought it lock, stock, and barrel, and moved in."

"And about a month later, I saw a Hallmark movie about a honeymoon destination resort, and that was that. It was fate!" Rose's hands waved animatedly, and her bracelets jangled happily.

"Did you leave family behind in New York?" Mark Wilder asked.

Ike took Rose's hand. "No. It's always just been the two of us. God didn't choose to bless us in that way."

"But we've had a long, wonderful marriage and now, all of you couples are our children!" Rose exclaimed. "And we so enjoy giving all of you the best start to your marriages that we can! It's our mission now."

I felt Rose's gaze boring into Brandon and me, and tried to send her a telepathic message. *If you have designs on fixing me up with this baboon, you're in for a disappointment, Rosie.*

6

LANDON RAN A finger under his collar. Ike and Rose had just finished their welcoming announcement to hearty applause. Despite his chagrin over the whole arrangement, Landon had to admire the older couple. What he had seen of the resort so far was beautiful, and they seemed in their element.

He found himself standing with the men and, too late, realized that the others were helping their wives to their feet. Miss Anderson stood on her own.

"We're going to take a moonlight walk through the gardens," Mark Wilder said. He looked at the two of them. "What about you?"

"I think we'll—ah, go back to the room," Landon responded quickly.

Mark produced an exaggerated wink and took his wife's hand. "I get you, man," he said to Landon. "This will be a short walk."

Great. All Landon could think about was getting out of this blasted penguin suit and relaxing in his room, *alone*. But

24

he'd given a completely different impression. He felt hot anger radiating off the woman next to him.

The Wilders and McFaddens murmured their goodbyes, and Ike and Rose materialized beside him. They were about a foot shorter than him, and really cute together. Landon was already developing a soft spot for them.

"Your rooms are on the same hallway," Rose said. "Alphabetical by the husband's last name. Singer and St. Fair. You're practically neighbors. The Smiths are between you."

Landon glanced down at Kelsea, who looked close to tears. *Her married name would have been Singer.* He felt a pang of sympathy. "Then let me walk you home," he offered. It was the least he could do in light of the carbs remark. Landon had no idea what had come over him.

Kelsea looked at him with a mild expression of surprise. Well, he *had* been pretty much an ogre to her to this point. This was no more her fault than his, and there was no reason to be unchivalrous. They said their goodbyes to the Goldmans and thanked them for their understanding and hospitality.

As soon as Rose and Ike were out of earshot, the lemon-sucking woman was back. "I can find my own way back to my room," she snapped.

For the love of Mike. "Since we're right next to each other, we may as well walk there together."

Her beautiful, dark eyes shot daggers at him. "Are you sure there's room? My carb-laden hips won't push you off the sidewalk?"

He felt lower than a dachshund. "I—"

"My hips are just fine. I'm perfectly proportioned and work hard to stay that way."

You sure are, he thought appreciatively. But that probably wasn't the right thing to say right now, either.

They began to walk. Kelsea looked up at him through her long, dark lashes. "I'm not sleeping with you, so don't get any ideas," she hissed.

Landon came to a full stop, and his jaw dropped. The nerve of the woman! *No wonder she's here alone.* "Don't flatter yourself, Miss Anderson!" he said through clenched teeth.

"I'm just making sure we're perfectly clear on that matter, Mr. St. Fair," she retorted.

Landon rolled his eyes. She sounded like a schoolmarm from the 1800s. "Believe me, that's the furthest thing from my mind," he muttered.

They walked in silence, and Kelsea kept her distance from him (no doubt to avoid catching his cooties). Landon imagined himself walking next to Nicola, who was nearly his height when she wore heels. Their arms would be wrapped around one another's waists, and they would probably stop every few steps for a kiss. Landon could hardly believe that all of that was in his past. He glanced down at Kelsea and, if the look on her face was any clue, figured that she was having similar thoughts.

"What's his name?" Landon asked softly.

Kelsea blinked, her deep brown eyes shiny with tears. *She really does have beautiful eyes,* Landon thought to himself. She swiped a hand across them. "Ryan," she whispered, barely audible.

They stopped at her door and she pulled a key card out of her little purse. Landon paused, and tried to think of something encouraging to say. "Well, it may not seem like it now, but you're probably better off without him."

Kelsea gasped, and her eyes flashed fire. "Says who? You don't know *anything,* Brandon St. Fair!" She swiped the key card and opened the door with an angry push.

"Hey, I'm sorry," Landon offered. "I didn't mean—"

The door closed in his face with a loud slam.

7

WHO DOES HE think he is? I threw another wadded tissue toward the wastebasket, and missed. *Who cares?* I couldn't even muster up the energy to get off the bed to pick it up.

Brandon St. Fair was by far the most exasperating human being on the face of the planet. As if he knew *anything* about my hips, or Ryan, or—just *anything!* And now it looked like I was going to be stuck with him for the next week, at least for meals. Maybe tomorrow I could find some food at a market and eat in my room. I looked around. No refrigerator, no microwave, no coffeemaker, no utensils of any kind. I wondered if I could subsist on fruit, nuts, and crackers for a week.

I let out a sigh. The owners were just the sweetest couple, and they could have refused to let me stay, or made things uncomfortable. I suppose I could put up with their one request and sit through meals with the insufferable man.

I changed into comfy sleep clothes and climbed into the king-sized bed. Compared to my single daybed at home, it felt as big as Texas, and compounded my sense of loneliness.

I tried in vain to chase images of Ryan from my mind, to forget how cherished I felt when he kissed me, and how safe and content I was when he held me. Now, I felt alone and bereft. I needed a distraction, but none of the books I'd brought held any interest.

I fired up my tablet and started absentmindedly surfing the net. The promotional info on the resort's website stated that internet service on the island was spotty, so I'd only brought it to watch movies on the plane, or so I told myself.

Before I knew it, my fingers had typed *Brandon St. Fair*. I clicked on some more keys and frowned. It appeared that he didn't have an online footprint. I found four men with that name, none of them remotely close to being him. None of them had his impressive height, his broad shoulders and trim waistline, the deep cleft in his chin, or his golden, dark blond hair. I had to admit that he filled out a tux in a way I'd seen on no other man.

Brandon St. Fair. For some reason, the name didn't sit right with me. He didn't really seem like a Brandon.

Why was I wasting time thinking about him? I started to go to Ryan's page, then remembered that I had made a pact with myself to stay off social media this week. He rarely updated it, anyway, and I had already unfriended him. I closed my computer and turned off the light.

I lay awake for a long time, unable to shut off my brain. I was still steaming about Brandon's carbs comment at dinner. Maybe I'd turn the tables at the next meal. Surely there was something…I ticked through his physical attributes and to my chagrin, couldn't think of anything that wasn't perfect. And of course I didn't know him well enough to come up with anything else.

Why did this guy get under my skin? *Stop thinking about him.*

I rolled over and punched my pillow. With nothing else to think about, my mind wandered back to Ryan. What had I done to make him cancel our wedding? Why did he stop loving me? How would I go on? I was almost thirty years old. I would just join a convent and become a nun. *Oh wait, I'm not Catholic.*

I started to cry. *Drat.* Now I was all stuffy and wouldn't be able to sleep. I switched on the light and went to find my nasal spray. It was with my toiletries on the bathroom counter.

As I reached for it, I spied the little black velvet box that held my engagement ring. Another piece of my splintered heart fell away. *My beautiful ring.* I opened the box and gently fingered the diamond. It wasn't an extravagant ring, but we'd chosen it together. Memories of that day flooded my senses, and tears rolled down my cheeks.

LANDON THREW HIS tux on the closet floor and hoped he wouldn't have to wear it again for a long, long time. The rest of the meals for the duration of the week were casual dress, and only the final night was formal. He had a pair of black dress slacks and a white dinner jacket that would do.

He scowled to himself. Miss Anderson was from the St. Louis area. What were the chances? She probably lived less than thirty minutes from him. Landon picked up his laptop and hopped online. He would have to be very careful not to give any clues away about himself. No way did he want her or anyone else knowing where he was from, or anything else about him.

Before he realized it, he had typed in *Kelsey Anderson, Kirkwood, Missouri*. One hit, but it sure wasn't her. But what was this? *Kelsea* Anderson. There she was, holding two Pomeranians. That was an unusual spelling of the name, but a pretty one. It suited her. *No relationship info to show.* She'd shed her affiliation with Ryan Singer quickly, as

Landon had with Nicola. Hometown, Kankakee, Illinois. No college listed. *Worked at St. Louis Zoo.* That was impressive.

He scrolled down. *Owner of Kelsea's Kritter Sitter Service.* In one click, he was on her business website. Dog walker and companion, pet (and/or house) sitter, plant waterer, personal shopper, errand girl. She'd been doing it for about a year and had a five-star rating from seventy-two clients. Well, that was just about the cutest thing he'd ever seen.

Landon found himself smiling as he scrolled through dozens of pictures of Kelsea with various animals, mostly dogs. She looked carefree, relaxed, and absolutely beautiful in her element, nothing like his shrewish dinner companion from tonight. Her long, luxurious dark brown hair hung in graceful layers, and her eyes sparkled with joy. This woman was clearly a compassionate animal lover.

And, as he had seen tonight in person, she had a tall, perfectly proportioned athletic figure and *really* nice legs.

Landon shook his head, and closed out of the website. *What am I doing? She's prickly as a cactus, totally exasperating, and after this week, I'll never have to see her again. St. Louis is big enough for both of us.*

He was just about to power down his computer when a thought flew into his mind. After a few clicks, he easily found Ryan Singer. He had dark hair and eyes, not unlike Kelsea's. Probably a couple of inches taller than her, and skinny. Software salesman for a national firm. Lifelong St. Louis resident. Graduate of SLUH (St. Louis University High) and UMSL. There was nothing remarkable until a few words jumped off the page. Landon winced. *In a relationship with Jenna Harmon.*

THE BREAKFAST BUFFET opened on the main patio at seven o'clock, and I had every intention of being there, even though I'd gotten little sleep. There was no reason why I couldn't come alone. I didn't need a babysitter, or Mr. Know-it-All's annoying company. It was unlikely that I'd run into Ike or Rose here. The resort owners would surely have things to keep them busy early in the day.

I gazed out over the expanse of white sand to the aqua waters beyond. *Perfect.* I'd go for a walk along the beach after breakfast, and then maybe go back to my room and take a nap.

The patio was nearly empty. *Well, duh, Kelsea. If you were here with Ryan, you'd probably find a reason to stay in the room, too.* My heart gave a painful squeeze. I wondered how long it would take to get over him.

Maybe it isn't really over, I mused as I sat down with a toasted English muffin and a bowl of fruit. I popped a bit of juicy mango into my mouth and closed my eyes. *Heavenly.* I hadn't had real fresh fruit in months.

I replayed my last conversation with Ryan in my head as I'd done a thousand times since. He'd come to my apartment last Tuesday night, and the moment I saw his face, I knew something was horribly wrong.

"I can't do this. I'm just not ready to settle down, Kels," he'd finally said.

"You're dumping me? We're through? Almost three years down the drain?" I'd practically screamed.

"No, no, not at all," Ryan said. "Just taking a step back. I don't know, maybe I'll be ready by next summer, or next year." His foot bounced nervously. "You had your heart set on a fall wedding anyway."

Yes, I did. It was your mother who wanted a winter wedding.

"Why, Ryan?" I'd begged, tears running down my cheeks. "Why are you doing this?"

He couldn't even look me in the eye. "I'm not even thirty yet, Kels. I just—I'm just not ready."

"So this is about the age difference again?" I was two and a half years older, and Ryan always found a reason to bring that up.

"No, it's not. I just need some space."

I've always hated that phrase. Along with *I'm taking a step back.*

He insisted that I keep the ring. "Who knows, we might, you know—need it in the future." That sounded lame, even to me.

As we stood at my door, tears ran down my cheeks, and my heart splintered into a million pieces. "Ryan, just tell me—is there someone else? Have you met someone else?"

He took my hands in his. "Kels, no, absolutely not. No way. Listen, I'll—I'll have my mom make all the calls, cancel everything, and I'll call you tomorrow." And with a dry, emotionless peck on my cheek, he was gone.

He never did call. But maybe I just need to give him some space.

"Good morning, Kelsea!" Rose's chipper voice brought me back to the present. She gave my shoulders a squeeze. "How did you sleep, dear?"

She was a pink ball of energy. Her pinkish-white hair was perfectly coiffed, sans the tiara. She wore pink capri pants, a brightly flowered shirt, and her Converse.

"I slept fine, Rose," I lied.

She sat down. "Remember, my friends call me Rosie."

"I slept fine, Rosie," I said, trying in vain to keep my voice steady.

She took my hand and squeezed. "And friends don't lie," she said softly. She pressed a paper napkin into my other hand.

I swiped it across my cheeks. "The room is beautiful, and the bed is so comfortable. I just—"

"You don't need to explain anything, dear. You've suffered a terrible loss. Just give yourself time to mourn, and before you know it, things will be better."

I couldn't speak, so I nodded, and drew in a deep breath.

"And you've chosen the best place to recover," she said. "The climate and the restorative power of nature will work its magic on you."

I gazed out at the pristine beach and sat up a little straighter. I was feeling better already. "I'm going to walk along the beach after breakfast. Thanks, Rosie."

"Did I ever tell you that I almost married another man before I met my Ike?"

I smiled to myself. When would she have told me that? I'd been in the woman's presence for less than two hours, surrounded by a group of people. "No, you didn't."

"His name was Tommy O'Houlihan. A Black Irish. You know what I mean by that, don't you?"

I nodded. "A TDH—tall, dark, and handsome."

Rose's laugh tinkled like a waterfall. She patted my hand again. "Oh my dear, yes. *Very* TDH, with jet black hair and the most piercing blue eyes that seemed to see all the way to my soul." She sighed. "So handsome. I met him at a dance, and it was love at first sight, for both of us." She giggled like a schoolgirl. "I was just eighteen, and he was twenty-five. Such a man of the world! We saw each other every day for the next two weeks, and he had grand plans. He wanted to marry me and take me back to Ireland with him!"

I gasped. "How romantic! But how could you have left your family?"

"Oh, honey, I would have gone to Mars with that man!" she chuckled.

I laughed with her. "But obviously, something happened," I ventured.

"Yes, well." Rose's expression turned serious. "Like I said, we were inseparable after we met. But Tommy was always busy at night. And he would never tell me what he was doing, just said he had to work."

"Uh, oh," I said.

"Uh, oh is right." Rose shook her head. "Turns out he was involved in a theft ring with a bunch of other Irishmen. They'd been riding high for almost four months, and were planning to culminate things with a huge robbery and then flee back to Ireland."

"How did you discover this?"

"My brother, George," Rose said. "He was a brand new beat cop, just twenty-three years old. To make a long story short, the Irish gang was already on his radar when I told him about Tommy, and it made George very nervous. Tommy called me one afternoon and said he needed to see me that night. He would be working but needed my help with something. George smelled a rat and followed me. It was a good thing he did. Tommy was going to use me as a decoy on their 'job' that night."

"Oh my, you could have been hurt, or even arrested."

She nodded. "It could have turned out very badly."

I squeezed her hand. "You must have been devastated."

"Oh, I was, my dear, I was inconsolable."

"Were you angry with George?"

"At first, yes, but then once I started thinking with my brain instead of my heart, I realized the amazing work he'd done to solve the case. I was so proud of him." Her face glowed. "He was promoted to detective the next year. My brother had an amazing and successful career with the NYPD for over forty years. He achieved the level of Assistant Police Commissioner." There was no mistaking Rose's pride in her brother's accomplishments.

"That's wonderful, Rosie."

"So you see, dear Kelsea, Ike wasn't my Plan A for marriage. He was my Plan B."

I just about jumped out of my seat. "Plan B? Did my mother put you up to this?" The words shot out of my mouth before I could stop them.

Rose's clear blue eyes reflected confusion. "Your mother? I've never met your mother, dear."

"No, no, of course you haven't, Rosie. I'm sorry. Forget I said that."

"I just meant that Tommy was Plan A, and after that fell through, I met Ike, and he was my Plan B, and so much better."

"I'm sure. You two seem very happy together."

"We are, and I'm sure you'll meet someone, too, and he'll be your Plan B, and it will be much better."

Or maybe Ryan will come to his senses, and I won't need a Plan B. "Well, I'm not ready for that just yet—"

Rose was looking past my shoulder. "Yoo hoo!" she trilled. "Over here, Mr. St. Fair!" She stood and waved.

Oh, no. My lovely morning, ruined. "Rosie, you don't need to go. Please, stay and tell me how you and Ike met."

"Oh, my dear, we'll save that for another time." I felt a dark cloud hovering behind me.

"Good morning, Mr. St. Fair!" Rose greeted him. "Isn't it a beautiful morning? Please, take a seat and keep Miss Anderson company. She looks so lovely this morning, doesn't she? We wouldn't want any of the married men to be tempted!" She giggled at her own joke.

"Good morning, ladies," Brandon's voice had an edge to it.

"Miss Anderson was just telling me that she wanted to walk along the beach," Rose said. "I'd appreciate it if you'd accompany her. We really don't want our female guests wandering around alone. You never know what kind of sharks are lurking about." She gave a little shiver.

What makes you think he isn't one of them? I bit my tongue. Brandon set his plate down but remained standing.

"I promise I'll do my best to protect her from harm," he said, taking Rose's hand and bending over it with a gallant kiss. It appeared the baboon had some manners, after all.

Rose giggled like a schoolgirl. "Oh, Mr. St. Fair! It's so rare to meet a real gentleman these days. Your mother must be so proud. Well, you two have a wonderful walk!" She pointed to her left. "Be sure to go all the way down to the cove. It's about two miles there and back, but well worth the walk. There are some beautiful shells there."

"Thank you, Rose. That sounds delightful," Brandon said. His voice had warmed up considerably.

Rose nearly skipped away. "Toodles!" she sang out.

LANDON HAD PURPOSELY come late to the breakfast buffet, secretly hoping that Kelsea would have already come and gone. She seemed like an early morning person, but obviously he rubbed her the wrong way, and he wasn't in the mood for her grousing. He'd filled his plate with all kinds of delicious looking food, but now that he'd seen her, he'd lost his appetite.

As soon as he sat down, she stood up. "I'm going for more fruit," she muttered.

Good. At least he could eat in peace, for a few minutes, anyway. He tucked into his eggs and waffles and nearly groaned with pleasure. He would need to make time to run every day if he wanted to fit into his clothes when he got home.

Miss Prickly Cactus returned, sat down, and dug into a bowl of berries without a word to him. She wasn't very chatty this morning, which was fine with him. Landon snuck a glance at her every once in a while, wondering if she had any idea that the man she was planning to marry less than a week ago was already with someone else. It made him feel just a little bit sorry for her. *I should lighten up on her just a bit.*

They continued eating in silence. Finally, she spoke.

"You're a gopher?" She gestured at his University of Minnesota hoodie. *Go, Golden Gophers!*

He didn't want to get into a bunch of personal details. "I'm from Minnesota." That was technically true.

"Figures."

He looked at her questioningly, and there was a mischievous light in her eye. "Gophers are rodents."

"And your point is?"

"Gophers are underground pests. In some tribal cultures, they're seen as a symbol of death."

"Charming, Miss Anderson. I wonder which animal *you* best represent."

She gave him a full-blown smile. *Beautiful, like the photos of her with the dogs.* "A lovely, graceful swan, of course!" She struck an elegant pose with her long, slender arms extended. "You heard Rose. I'm sure she would agree with me."

"Ha!" Brandon finished cleaning his plate, leaned back, and stretched out his legs. "You're a porcupine."

"A porcupine!"

"Yes. Also a rodent. One that has sharp quills or spines to keep predators away." He grinned at her. "They also have a fat, flat nose."

Kelsea's hand flew to her face. "I have a nice nose!" She ran her fingers over it.

Landon couldn't help but laugh. "Yeah, you do. But you've got some prickly quills, too." He looked at her evenly.

She stood. "Well, if I do, then I don't need a protector to walk along the beach."

Landon got to his feet. "No way are you going by yourself. With my luck, you'd get attacked by some hungry sea animal and Rose and Ike would never forgive me." He rubbed his stomach. "Besides, I've got to walk off that breakfast."

11

THERE WAS SOMETHING different about Brandon this morning, but I couldn't put my finger on it. He seemed a bit softer around the edges, less annoying. The banter about the gopher and porcupine was almost a little fun.

The walk down to the cove was beautiful, and I felt the stress ebbing away. I'd been wound tight as a coiled spring for the last five days. I knew Rose was right. This lovely setting was going to restore my equilibrium, or at least put me on the right path. Despite all the drawbacks, I was starting to think I'd made the right decision to come.

Brandon seemed lost in his thoughts as I was in mine, and neither of us said very much during our walk. It was a relief to not have to defend myself or put out the energy to make conversation. Best of all, the beach was deserted. None of the bridal couples was out this morning. I shouldn't have been surprised.

I wondered what Ryan was doing right now. If I had my phone with me, I'd be tempted to text him. I was so disappointed that he hadn't called me before I left St.

Louis. He'd promised. *He also promised to marry you, but didn't.*

I looked over at Brandon. His hands were jammed in the pockets of his cargo shorts, and his expression was vacant. I wondered what he was thinking. "Have you talked with her since it happened?" I asked.

"Her? You mean *her?*"

I nodded. "What's her name?" I figured he knew Ryan's name, why shouldn't I know hers?

His eyes grew cold. "It doesn't matter. She's in my past now."

"I'm sorry," I said. I couldn't think of anything else to say.

"Did Ryan leave you standing at the altar?"

"No," I replied. "We were supposed to get married Saturday afternoon, on New Year's Day, and he backed out the Tuesday night before."

Brandon didn't respond to that. We kept walking. When we got to the cove, we decided to take off our sandals and put our feet in the clear, turquoise water.

"Oh, it's so warm!" I exclaimed. "It'll be even better later when the sun starts to heat up." I did a little jig in the water and twirled around and around. "This is heaven!"

That elicited a smile from Brandon. Then he just stood there, looking out at the ocean. Pretty soon, the smile faded from his face.

"She left me at the altar."

"Like, literally standing at the altar, waiting for her? Like in the movies?"

"Exactly. In front of five hundred guests."

I gasped. "Oh, my. That's—that's—terrible. I can't even think of a word for it."

"Humiliating," he said, his voice flat.

"Did you have the slightest notion beforehand?"

He kicked up one foot and splashed a little water. "Not up here," he said, pointing at his head, "but yeah, in here." He tapped his fist over his heart. "We'd—things hadn't been great since Thanksgiving. I just chalked it up to the holidays and all the stress of the wedding. I thought it would be fine after all of it was over. She and her mother were—*are*—pretty high-strung women."

"I'm not high strung," I said. "At least I don't think I am. Our wedding was pretty small. Nowhere close to five hundred guests."

"Was it hard canceling all your arrangements? I'm sure you lost all your deposits."

For the first time in a while, I smiled. "I have no idea. Ryan's mother made all the arrangements, so I suppose she canceled them. Any lost deposits are hers."

Brandon's mouth tipped up in a small smile. "Sounds like you dodged a bullet."

I rolled my eyes. "You have no idea. That's the one silver lining in this cloud." But then I sighed. "I still have no idea why Ryan backed out. He insisted there's no one else, just said he needs some space. So I'm going to give it to him, and then hopefully we'll work things out."

"I wouldn't count on it," Brandon mumbled.

"There you go again!" I threw up my hands. "Expressing an opinion about something that you have *no* idea about!" I marched up the sand and grabbed my sandals. "I'm going back to my room."

I walked away without another word. After about a minute, I turned and looked over my shoulder. Brandon was still standing ankle-deep in the water, exactly where I'd left him, staring out to sea.

12

LANDON KNEW HE should have kept his mouth shut, but he couldn't help it. He was actually hoping to guide Kelsea to a frame of mind where she might be open to the possibility that her Ryan wasn't the model boyfriend, or fiancé, that she thought he was.

Why do I even care? He walked around in the little cove for a while, then collected his footwear and started up the beach. Kelsea was nowhere to be seen in front of him. *Good. She can take care of herself.*

Landon went back to his room and lasted about ten minutes. It was one thing to say that he'd just keep to himself there, but he found that he couldn't stay cooped up in the pink, romantic-themed room. And after more than two months of bitterly cold weather, he craved being outdoors in the warm sunshine and gentle breezes.

He wandered outside to a cobbled path meandering through some gardens. Soon, he rounded a corner and almost smacked into a couple entwined in a passionate embrace. *Great.* Landon scooted around them and kept going.

He went around another corner, and there was Kelsea sitting alone on a bench. Her face twisted into a scowl when she saw him. "Oh, it's you."

Landon figured that somewhere in the universe, someone must be praying for patience on his behalf. He decided to take the high road. "I tried to stay in my room, but couldn't. It's just too beautiful out here."

She shrugged. "Yeah, me, too."

Landon looked up as he heard male and female laughter approaching. *Oh no.* It was the McFaddens.

"Top o' the morning, St. Fairs!" Julie McFadden cried. She acted like they were long-lost best friends. Both hers and her husband's eyes darted between Landon and Kelsea. They were no doubt wondering why they weren't wrapped around one another like every other couple. "Isn't this beautiful! We're beginning to see why this is called the Island of Gardens."

Landon stepped over to the bench and sat down next to Kelsea. *In for a penny, in for a pound.* He wrapped his hand loosely around hers. If she was going to protest, she'd have to make a public spectacle of it.

"Yes, we enjoyed a walk on the beach earlier," Landon said. "If you head west for about two miles, there's a beautiful cove." *And it'd be great if you went there right now.*

"We'll have to remember that!" Julie's head rested on her husband's chest, and his arm held her close. "So, what's your favorite thing about the resort so far?"

"The food," Kelsea responded quickly. "Except of course that I have to watch my carbs."

Landon gave her hand a little squeeze. "I apologized

for my insensitive remark, love bug." He tried to laugh lightheartedly, but it came out sounding strained.

"Yes, you did, sweetness," Kelsea said through clenched teeth.

Brian McFadden looked at Landon. "I think this one's gonna cost you a piece of jewelry," he said with a laugh.

His wife's normally happy eyes flashed. "Not every problem can be solved with a piece of jewelry, dear."

To Landon's shock, Kelsea scooted closer, laid her head on his shoulder, and laced her long, slender fingers through his. "I shouldn't have brought it up again. He already made it up to me last night, in all the ways that count," she sighed.

Landon felt heat crawling up his neck. "Ah—well, let's just keep those details in the, um, family." He cleared his throat. If the McFaddens weren't going to leave, Landon would take control. He hauled Kelsea to her feet and stood, keeping a grip on her hand.

"Well, then, we'll let you enjoy your walk. Nice talking with you," he murmured, and set off, dragging Kelsea with him.

Once they were well out of earshot, she stopped, and peeled her hand from his. "You can give me my hand back now," she said in a flat voice.

"Gladly," Landon retorted. "Why did you have to bring the carbs comment up again? Can we just let it rest?"

"You started it," she shot back.

"And I said I was sorry," he retorted.

"When? I don't remember that."

Landon rolled his eyes and crossed his arms in front of him. "Fine. I'm sorry."

"Thank you." She looked so prim and proper. An evil little voice whispered into Landon's ear.

"I'm sorry carbs go straight to your hips," he said. "Kidding! I'm kidding!" He immediately added with a laugh.

But it was too late. Kelsea's eyes boiled over with anger. "You're—you're insufferable, Brandon St. Fair!" she shouted. "If they crossed a gopher with a baboon, *you* would be the result!" She spun on her heel and marched off.

13

THE NEXT MORNING, I was one of the first ones down to breakfast again. No matter what, I was going to eat a meal without the odious company of the Gopher Baboon. I couldn't decide whether to call him a *Goboon* or a *Babpher*. Neither one really rolled off the tongue.

The weather was exactly the same today as it was yesterday, that is to say, it was perfect. The temperature, the breeze, the sun. Absolutely perfect, and mesmerizing. I would find a way to spend every moment outdoors.

"Are you finished?" I came out of my reverie to see a guy looming over me, a towel slung over his shoulder, one arm balancing a plastic tub on his hip.

I took the last sip of freshly squeezed OJ and nodded. "Yeah, that's fine." I stood to leave.

"I'm Todd." He took a step closer into my personal space, and I felt his eyes roving over me. He lowered his voice to a whisper. "I heard that you're here alone, without a husband." Then I noticed his dark, good looks. His coloring was similar to Ryan's, but he was broader, more muscular, a little like Brandon. He had arresting blue eyes.

I glanced around, but it appeared that we were alone. My heart rate sped up, and I took a step back. "I'm—"

He touched a fingertip to my left hand and tossed out a lazy smile. "Looks like you're not wearing a ring. There's no reason for you to be lonely here, sugar." I recoiled as his fingers trailed up my arm. Todd didn't know it, but a vital part of his anatomy was about two seconds away from a decisive encounter with my knee.

"Is there a problem here, sweetheart?" A voice came from just behind me, and Brandon's arm came firmly around my shoulder. He wore tennis shoes, khaki shorts, and a long-sleeved navy cotton pullover with the sleeves pushed up. As much as I didn't want to, I felt myself leaning into his solid, muscular strength.

"Ah—no. No problem at all." I laid my palm lightly on his chest and did my best to smile and look casual. "I was just finishing breakfast." My heart slowed down a little. "And—waiting for you." He moved his hand down to settle around my waist and pulled me a little closer.

"Well, that's good," Brandon said, his gaze locked on Todd, "because I know Ike and Rose wouldn't be happy if they heard there was a problem." His words were innocent enough, but the message was crystal clear.

"I must have been mistaken," Todd said to me. Then he pasted on a brittle smile and began to back away. "You two enjoy the day."

Brandon's annoyed gaze followed the man as he nearly ran back inside the building. "What was that all about?"

I dropped my hand and took a step back. "Nothing to

concern yourself with," I said, aiming for a light tone. "He was just being friendly."

"He was leering at you," he muttered.

"I can take care of myself, Brandon. I'm not your responsibility." I crossed my arms in front of me.

He ran a hand through his hair. "I know you're not my responsibility. It just looked like—that he was—you know, trying to—" He let out an audible sigh. "You know what? I'm done." He held out one arm like a stop sign and began to back away. "Best of luck to you, Kelsea. I won't bother you again." He turned and strode away, his long, muscular legs eating up the distance.

I was so stunned, I couldn't speak, couldn't move. *You're really making a mess of this.* I ran after him. "Brandon, wait!" He slowed as I caught up with him. I tugged on his elbow and scooted around to face him.

"I—yes, he was—invading my—personal space," I said haltingly. To my embarrassment, I felt my eyes begin to well up, and I wrapped my arms protectively around my middle. "I—he, he asked if I was here alone, and told me that he'd be happy to appease my loneliness."

Brandon's hands rested loosely on his hips. I don't know what kind of reaction I expected, but it sure wasn't the devastating smile that transformed his face. "Well, I'm one ahead of you. A maid greeted me when I came out of my room this morning and made me a similar offer. Then, before I even got down here, another woman cornered me in the hallway." He shook his head. "I'm pretty sure *her* proposition is illegal in some states. And if you can believe it, I think she's one of the happy newlyweds." His voice dripped with irony.

I was so miserable, but the absurdity of it hit me, and I couldn't help but giggle. I brushed away a tear. "The last thing I expected when I came here alone was to have to fend off some creep. So, what did you say to those women?"

"I neither confirmed nor denied the allegation that I was here alone," Brandon said, and then seemed to back pedal. "I mean, I didn't say anything. I walked away from both of them."

It's always hard for me to admit when I'm wrong, but I needed to step up. I took a breath. "Thank you for coming to my rescue. I mean it. I don't think he really meant me any harm, but it was getting uncomfortable."

Brandon's gaze flicked down to my feet and back up to my eyes, but for some reason it didn't bother me the way it had when I felt Todd appraising me. "I'm sure you would have handled it," he said firmly, "but I couldn't help myself. I'm too old-fashioned. I can't resist a beautiful lady in distress." He smiled again, and I felt the breath leave me.

He looked around, and gestured toward the shore. "I was just going to take a walk along the beach, in the other direction," he said. "Join me?"

For once, words escaped me, so I simply nodded.

When he smiled, Brandon St. Fair was really a very handsome man, if you liked that type. Which I didn't.

14

BY THE TIME they returned from their walk, Landon and Kelsea had made a pact. In his mind, Landon knew it made sense, like a good business deal. After the tumult of the last several days, both of them craved solitude to lick their wounds and sort through their feelings. But in the present setting, even the hint of being there unattached was apparently going to attract the wrong kind of attention, so they decided to stick together in public. Pretty soon, the rumors would die down.

They made it back just before the buffet closed. Landon ate every bite of his breakfast, which, like every meal, was superb.

Kelsea nibbled on some grapes. "You know, I was thinking about what you said about knowing 'in here' that your fiancée was going to back out." She tapped her fingers on her chest. "I was completely shocked when Ryan came to see me, but in retrospect, things had been a little off since Thanksgiving."

"Did you ask him about it?"

"Yeah, and he said things were just wild at work with year-end stuff, and he was trying to get ready to be gone on our honeymoon."

"You want more coffee?" Landon asked. Kelsea shook her head.

"I still can't believe you threw your watch in the ocean," she said.

He shrugged. "You were right. We're on island time. No watching the clock."

She laughed. "But I didn't mean that you should destroy a perfectly beautiful watch! It looked brand new."

"It *was* brand new. It was an early wedding gift." He pushed back his chair and stood.

Kelsea stopped and looked at him, a grape in midair. "Oh...I get it."

Landon nodded, and slipped his hands into his pockets. "There was no reason to keep it. So thanks for ridding me of it. You ready?"

She nodded and stood, and they started walking.

"You could have sold it, you know. Made some money off it."

He frowned. "It was engraved."

"Oh." Kelsea didn't seem to have a response for that. A movement ahead caught her attention, and she pointed. "Hey, what's going on over there?" Rose and Ike were just outside the entrance to the main building. Ike handed Rose a bullhorn.

"Good morning, lovebirds!" her cheery voice rang out. "For anyone who wants to go shopping in town, the shuttle buses will leave in ten minutes. We'll be back in time for lunch." She began to put the bullhorn down, and then spied them. "Yoo hoo! Kelsea and Brandon! I hope you'll come shopping with us."

Great. Landon would rather have his teeth pulled out without Novocain than go shopping. Hopefully Kelsea would want to go back to her room, so he could go hide in his.

To his great disappointment, she waved gaily and called out, "We'd love to come, thanks!"

15

"WHY'D YOU DO that?" Brandon glowered at me. "I don't want to go shopping."

I grimaced. "Oh, I'm sorry," I said. "I just thought of something I really need to get. You don't have to come."

He threw up his hands. "It'll draw attention if you go alone," he said. "Remember, the whole point is to stick *together* so we don't stick *out*."

"You're right, you're right," I said. "My mind is somewhere else. I need to get something out of my room before the bus leaves." I hurried toward the door that led to our corridor, and Brandon followed.

"I'll grab my wallet," he muttered.

We made our way back to the shuttle buses, which were filling up quickly. I slipped into a seat, and Brandon lowered himself down beside me. The day was starting to heat up, and he'd shed his cotton hoodie. He wore a dark gray t-shirt that clung to his athletic torso.

Holy guacamole. Ryan ran some and rode a bike occasionally, but didn't lift weights or anything. He was more soft than hard, and I always said I didn't really like muscles on guys. I was going to have to rethink that.

"So, what do you need to buy?" Brandon asked. The aroma of wintergreen floated over on his breath.

"I'll tell you later," I whispered.

The scenery on the drive was beautiful, and we enjoyed looking at it together out the window. Brandon's arm rested lightly on the seat back, and I found that I wasn't completely repulsed when he leaned closer occasionally to get a better look.

When we reached the center of town, Molli announced that the shuttle buses would depart for the return trip in exactly two hours.

Brandon and I loitered on the sidewalk until the others had moved away. "Where to?" he asked.

"The nearest pawn shop."

"Pawn shop? What do you need with a pawn shop?"

"I'm selling this." I drew out the black velvet box and opened it.

"Wow. You want to sell your engagement ring?"

I nodded. "Ryan said I could keep it. What am I going to do with it? If he comes crawling back, he can buy me another one. A bigger one." Everything that seemed so heartbreaking at night felt different in the morning sun. "And, I need the money to buy a wedding band."

Brandon's features twisted in confusion. "Wedding band?"

"Yes, just a cheap one." I held up my left hand. "Sleazy Todd pointed out that I wasn't wearing a ring."

Brandon nodded. "Good thinking. I should get one, too."

"You don't need one. Lots of married men don't wear a ring."

He smiled. "Just the one through their nose."

"Ha, ha," I retorted, and punched him playfully on the arm. It was rock solid. *Wow.*

Brandon started walking. "Come on. Let's find a jewelry store. You'll get a better deal there than from a pawn shop."

The proprietor of the fourth store finally met Brandon's high standards, and made a more than fair offer. Once that transaction was finished, we asked to see the least expensive wedding bands.

"Cheap? Why you want cheap?" The man pointed to me and smiled broadly at Brandon. "Your woman worth the best gold."

Brandon and I looked at each other and laughed. "She's not—it's a long story," he said.

"Trust us, cheap ones will be fine," I added with a smile.

The man held his hand up and pointed. "You no want fingers turn green," he said in his parlance. "I have what you need, make you good deal."

"You can show us something a little nicer." Brandon looked down at me. "I'm buying both bands."

"You are not!" I exclaimed. "I'm buying my own."

Brandon looked at the store owner. "Would you excuse us for a moment?" He took my elbow and guided me away.

"Look, Kelsea, let me buy these. I can afford it, and they won't be that much."

I crossed my arms in front of me. "I'm not poor, Brandon." *Liar.*

He raised his eyebrows. "You said you had to sell your engagement ring to buy this."

"I'm not taking charity." *I'm poor, but proud.*

Brandon sighed. "Look, just consider it an investment on my part. I'll buy the pair, then sell them back in the States after this week is over. I won't lose any money on them, I'll probably even make a little."

I tapped my foot nervously and considered it. I could really use the ring money to make up for the commissions I was losing from being gone this week. I had spent nearly every penny of my savings on this trip, and I didn't get a paid vacation like Ryan would have, or no doubt like Brandon was getting. I had no idea what he did for a living, but it seemed like he was doing just fine.

I nodded curtly. "Oh, all right."

"Good." Brandon smiled and led me back to the counter, where the man waited. Ten minutes later, we left wearing matching tri-gold bands. I had never seen rose gold and thought the combination was lovely.

We did some window shopping for the duration, and Brandon waited patiently while I picked up a couple of pairs of nicer shorts and shirts to replace the slouchy clothes I'd brought from home. Not that I was trying to impress…anyone, but the bargain prices were too good to pass up.

When we sat down on the bus, Brandon leaned over and touched my ring. "You know what this means, don't you?"

I eyed him warily. "I'm still not sleeping with you." I gasped. "Is that why you bought these? So I would sleep with you?"

He looked around nervously. "Shhh!"

I looked around, too. "No one is listening to us. They're literally wrapped up in each other," I said crossly.

"Of course that's not why I bought these. I was just kidding around," he said. The bus pulled away from the curb. "Pull in your quills, Miss Porcupine."

"Mr. Gopher, harbinger of death," I muttered.

16

LANDON AND KELSEA met a nice couple from San Francisco at dinner the next evening. Steve Isaacs turned out to be a big sports fan, and Landon thoroughly enjoyed their discussion. Every once in a while, he caught snippets of the women's conversation about fashion, cooking, and reality TV. At least Missy Isaacs was talking. Kelsea was making monosyllabic comments, and appeared to be more interested in his and Steve's conversation.

"Whoa, whoa there," she interrupted when Landon commented how impressed he was with Denver's new quarterback. "That guy wouldn't have had a snowball's chance in the devil's man cave of getting any playing time if Thompson hadn't been injured. He can't hit the broad side of a barn. JoJo Collins is the only one who can catch him. JoJo's the only reason the Broncos are still in the running."

Landon looked at her in amazement and hardly heard Steve's comment. Kelsea cited some stats, and Landon challenged her. She held out her hand. "Give me your phone."

Landon started to hand it over, then raised one eyebrow and raised his chin a notch.

"Pretty please?" she replied with a saccharine smile and flutter of eyelashes.

At that point, Landon would have given her anything she asked for.

She snatched the phone from his outstretched hand and searched until she found what she was looking for. "Ha! Read it and weep!" Landon had to admit that she was right.

She, Steve, and Landon sat chatting for another half hour, moving from football to hockey, and finally baseball. Having grown up in northern Illinois, Kelsea was an avowed Cubs fan. She said she didn't know much about hockey, but had been to a Blues game in St. Louis and enjoyed it more than she thought she would. Landon wished he could take her to a game. He'd grown up playing hockey, and imagined that once he shared his expert knowledge with her, she'd really get into it, screaming her head off. Landon watched as she said something to Steve about her beloved Cubbies. Her voice was animated, her eyes sparkled, and her hands waved around excitedly.

Missy didn't have anything to add to the conversation, and sat admiring her nails and looking bored. She was a beautiful blonde and reminded him a little of Nicola. Then it occurred to Landon that if Nicola had been sitting next to him tonight instead of Kelsea, she would have been chatting Missy up about fashion and reality TV. She didn't care about sports at all. He took her to a Blues game once, but she complained about the noise so much that they left after about thirty minutes.

Missy Isaacs had finally had enough. "I'm ready for a

walk in the moonlight, Steve," she pouted as she leaned up and kissed his cheek.

He jumped up and helped her to her feet. "Sure thing, honey." Landon stood to shake Steve's hand. "It was great meeting you folks," Steve said with a smile. "I hope we'll see you again."

"Likewise," Landon said. He waited until the Isaacs left and then looked at Kelsea. "You're quite a sports fan." He sat down again.

"I am," she replied. "Does that surprise you?"

"I never really thought about it one way or the other until you joined the conversation."

She frowned. "Did that upset you?"

"No. Why would it?"

She didn't respond. Landon smiled at her. "You made some really great points. I've just never— I've never dated a woman who could hold her own talking about stats and players and all of that. Not that we're dating," he quickly added. "I just, well, you know."

Kelsea still didn't say anything. Her mind seemed to be somewhere else. "Ryan wasn't into sports as much as I am. If we were out with friends and a discussion like this one tonight started up, he didn't have much to contribute, so he'd just play on his phone and then after we'd get home he'd sulk and accuse me of trying to show him up in public." She pursed her lips. "I think he wanted me to just sit there and look gorgeous like Missy."

Landon let out a soft snort. "Missy isn't gorgeous. She wears too much makeup. She'd be prettier if she stuck to her natural look, like you." He scooted back his chair. "You ready?"

"Like me?" Kelsea looked surprised as she stood. "Don't men want their women looking sexy and exotic?"

Landon frowned at her. "Well, yeah, on special occasions. But if she looks that way all the time, it's not special. And the time it takes to put all of that on! My fiancée would take an hour and a half to get ready to go out for thirty minutes. She didn't have to look like a goddess to make a Target run." They were outside now. "You wanna go for a walk in the moonlight?"

Kelsea eyed him warily. "Sure, I'll walk with you. But we'll talk about the last time the Twins and the Cardinals were in a playoff series. No romance, because, you know, I'm not—"

"Yeah, yeah, I get it. You're not sleeping with me. You don't have to keep saying it. My ego has been beaten down enough lately."

She crossed her arms in front of her. "I'm not trying to beat down your ego," she said with an edge to her voice. "I just don't sleep around."

"And you think I do?" Landon shot back. He'd had just about enough of this.

"I don't know. I don't know you well enough. But you're a man."

"You're right. I'm a man. A man who was literally dumped in the most humiliating way possible, in front of five hundred people, most of them strangers. But some of them were my family, friends, and professional contacts and colleagues. And you don't know me well enough to form an opinion about my sleeping habits, or anything else."

Kelsea had the grace to look embarrassed, and truly repentant. "I'm sorry, Brandon. You're absolutely right, and that was insensitive of me. I'm sorry."

He stood there with his hands jammed in his pockets. "Thanks." He looked at the ground and then back to her. "Could we--would you just walk with me for a little while, please? And just not say anything?'

She nodded, and followed him.

It was a beautiful night for a walk on the beach. The sights, sounds, and smells were intoxicating. Landon was finally starting to relax. They walked for almost fifteen minutes without talking.

"Nicola."

"What?"

"Her name was Nicola." We met a little over two years ago at a social event."

"You mean a party?"

"Well, it was a kind of—you know, a business thing. They really don't call them parties." Landon didn't want to reveal that he attended most of these events as a representative of the law firm. Or that he'd made partner after landing the DiCarlo Luxury Motors account.

"Well, I wouldn't know about that," Kelsea said. "Anyway, go on. What did she look like?"

"What did she look like?" he parroted.

"Yeah, you know. Is she a blonde? Brunette? Redhead? Tall? Short? Skinny? Fat?"

"Um, well, she's blonde. Taller than you. And skinnier." Before Kelsea could react, he corrected himself. "Too skinny, I told her that all the time. She could have used some of your curves."

Kelsea's eyes narrowed just a bit. "I think there's a compliment somewhere in there. Eyes?"

"Yes, she has eyes."

"Ha, ha."

"Dark eyes. She's Italian."

"Ah, Italiano, very interesting."

"Yes. Her family—they're very well off, her father is a very successful businessman. Owns a whole fleet of luxury car dealerships."

"What do you drive?"

Landon laughed. "Nothing close to a luxury car. I think I was getting one for a wedding gift, though."

"I thought she got you that watch."

"She did. The car would have been from her parents."

"Bummer."

He couldn't help but laugh. "Yeah, bummer."

"Is she older or younger than you?"

Landon frowned. "Two years younger. I'll be thirty-one in a few weeks."

"When?"

"On the 28th."

"No way! That's my birthday, too!" Kelsea winced. "It's the big three-oh for me."

What were the chances? One in about 365. "You're kidding, right?"

"Why would I kid about that? My birthday is January 28."

Landon couldn't think of anything to say.

"Ryan's younger than me. He said that he wasn't even thirty yet and wasn't ready to settle down. Do you think the age difference had something to do with it?"

Landon thought a moment. "It shouldn't. I've dated older women before—not by much, but a year or two. I think culture is more a factor than age."

"Culture, how so?"

"Well, I think that was one thing that drove Nicola and me apart. Her Italian heritage was so important to her, to all of them. It was just one more way that I didn't fit in. I always felt like an outsider."

"That's interesting," Kelsea said. "That was never the case for Ryan and me. I guess we're both just Heinz 57, you know, a mix."

Landon smiled at that description. "Nicola has a twin brother, Francisco, and he never accepted me, never thought I was good enough for her. If I'd been Italian, I might have stood a fighting chance. He was always telling her how this friend or that friend of his would have been a better match for her."

"And all his friends are Italian?"

"Oh, yeah. There's a very tight Italian community in— where we live."

Kelsea frowned. "And where is it that you live?"

"I didn't say." Landon smiled.

"I know, that's why I'm asking." She smiled back.

Landon wasn't ready to play that card yet. Maybe he never would be. "It doesn't matter. Anyway, when I realized Nicola had left the wedding, I knew she'd gone with Francisco. Her father confirmed it. It was probably Francisco's idea."

"They're really close, then?"

Landon nodded. "Oh, yeah. I guess it's that twin bond."

"I have a sister, Morgan," Kelsea said. "She's two years younger than me. We're close, but not crazy close like twins. What about you?"

"You mean siblings? Well, I'm not a twin, but I'm an *Irish* twin."

"You don't look Irish!" Kelsea laughed. "Wait! I've heard of Irish twins. But I can't remember what it means."

Landon smiled. "Yeah, I'm not Irish, I'm mostly Scandinavian. Irish twins are siblings born less than a year apart. *True* Irish twins are born in the same calendar year, and that was the case for us. I was born on January 28, and my brother arrived on December 24."

"Wow, that's crazy! Is it just the two of you?"

"No, we have an older sister and a younger sister." Landon was through giving personal information. "You ready to head back?"

Kelsea nodded, and they walked the whole way back in companionable silence, lost in their own thoughts. Landon couldn't believe it. They'd spent the whole evening together without one argument.

17

WHEN I GOT back to my room, I got ready for bed and opened my computer. Brandon St. Fair was certainly an enigma. I typed in *Nicola* and *Francisco*. Nothing. Then I entered the names with various permutations of *luxury car,* but that didn't get any hits either.

I typed his name in with the birthdate and year, and still nothing. There were websites where you could pay to find out more information about someone, but it sure wasn't worth it to me to fork out any dough.

Why do you even care? I scolded myself. After this week, I'd never see Brandon again. I looked at the background on my screen, a picture of Ryan and me that I hadn't bothered to change. *My mother was right. We would have given her beautiful grandchildren.* This made me even more melancholy. I quickly got back online and substituted it with a generic picture of a sunset.

After we'd finished lunch, Brandon and I had met Ike in the lobby. He was pinning a photo up on a bulletin board. "This is our brag board," he said with a chuckle. "Rosie likes to put up letters from all our couples, and Christmas cards that they send us, and baby announcements. We just got a Christmas card from the Jensens. Look at that, they were here just over a year ago, and now they have a little boy."

A tear rolled down my cheek. I'd probably never be able to send Rose and Ike a card with my children's picture on it.

18

THE NEXT MORNING'S walk turned into a run. Landon was impressed that Kelsea kept up with him, and told her so.

"I'm not short," she protested. "I'm five seven."

"I know, but I've got nine inches on you. Did you run track?" They were now back at the patio, enjoying the last of the breakfast buffet.

She nodded. "In high school. And I played lacrosse."

"I've never played lacrosse," he said. "But I played—"

Kelsea held up her hand. "No, no, wait. Let me guess." She eyed him. "Football and hockey."

Landon was surprised. "How'd you know?"

She shrugged. "You totally seem like a football jock, but you've had a broken nose, and you're from Minnesota, so I put two and two together."

"Good thinking. Why didn't you guess basketball?"

"You don't have the build," she said without hesitation. "Basketball players are tall, but lean."

"Oh, so now I'm fat?

"No, but you're—you have muscles."

She averted her eyes and was suddenly all into her cup of yogurt. And was she a little pink? Landon wanted to laugh out loud, and at the same time he was extremely flattered. He'd let it pass, for now. "I also swam," he said.

"Competitively?"

"Yes."

"What were your events?"

"Butterfly, breaststroke, and relay."

Kelsea chewed and seemed to be thinking about something. "I challenge you," she finally said. "Butterfly."

"Really? You won't mind getting your hair wet?"

Kelsea sputtered. "Are you kidding? Brandon, it's water. It dries." He couldn't believe it. Nicola couldn't even stand to be splashed with a few drops at the pool.

"You're on," he said with a smile.

Landon beat her in each of their three races, but she was good, and it was by no means a steal. It turned out she had been on the swim team in high school. He liked her competitive spirit, and she was a gracious loser.

They were now sitting in lounge chairs by the pool. Kelsea was wearing a one-piece red suit that was, in Landon's opinion, hotter than any bikini he'd ever seen. Red was definitely her color.

"If you don't mind my asking, where did you and Ryan meet?"

"Hmm. It's kind of a complicated story, and there are still some things about it that bother me."

"Maybe talking about it would help you sort it all out in your mind."

She stared at him for several seconds and then nodded. "Well, about three and a half years ago I moved to St. Louis. It was the first time I'd ever left home. I'm from Kankakee, Illinois."

"You didn't go away to college?" Of course, Landon already knew this from looking at her online profile.

Kelsea shook her head. "Well, I tried it, but it didn't stick. After dropping out of community college, I worked at a daycare—no thanks! —and went to beauty school." He couldn't help but smile.

"I cut hair for two years and got tired of standing on my feet in one place all day, so I gave that up. Next was a string of office temp jobs—*yawn*. After that, I started volunteering at a local animal shelter, where I adopted two Pomeranians, Sheldon and Penny."

"Cute."

"They are! They're my babies. But volunteering didn't pay—literally—so I got a job at a library. I'm an avid reader, so I thought that would be fun. It wasn't. Turns out I can't go hours on end without talking."

Landon looked at her with amusement. "You don't say?"

Kelsea smiled. "Well, yeah. So, I was still living at home. My dad died when I was twelve, and my sister Morgan had already gone away to college and then to grad school, and hadn't lived at home in years. So it was just Mom and me, and she was constantly harping on me about getting married and giving her grandchildren, and she's an elementary teacher, and she tried to set me up on a blind date with a second-grade teacher at her school, Percy Parker."

Landon laughed. "Sounds like a winner."

Kelsea shook her head. "Desperate times call for desperate

measures. I was still volunteering at the animal shelter, and saw an ad in a trade magazine for an entry-level opening at the St. Louis Zoo. I did a Skype interview and got hired."

Of course, Landon already knew this, too. "Wow, that's impressive. That's one of the best zoos in the country."

"I know. I couldn't believe that I was going to work there. So Sheldon and Penny and I moved to St. Louis to get away from my mother and Percy Parker, and after a few months, I started working in the petting zoo area, you know, where all the little kids get to come in and pet the animals. I totally loved it. It was so much fun talking with the kids and seeing them get so excited about the animals. And one Saturday afternoon, this family came in, a mom and a dad and their little girl. She was about three. Absolutely adorable."

Landon cringed. "Don't tell me."

"Yes, it was Ryan. But it wasn't what it looked like. Anyway, she was really into the animals and I probably spent about ten minutes with them, and they asked a lot of questions, and *he* asked a lot of questions, and asked my name, and was really nice, and said that their names were Ryan and Ashley and Brooke. And then they left." I sighed. "And then it got kind of sketchy."

Landon decided not to comment.

"So about a half hour later, I hear a guy call my name, and I turned around, and it was him. The dad of this little girl, or so I thought. And I said something like, 'Oh hi, did you forget something?' and he said, 'Well, yeah, I forgot to ask you what time you get off, and to ask if you would have dinner with me.' He was a total flirt."

"Yikes," Landon said. He couldn't wait to see how the story ended.

"So I was *completely* blown away, just in shock, and I said, 'Well, don't you think your *wife* would mind?' and then he said, 'Oh, she's not my wife, she's my girlfriend, and the kid's not mine.'"

Landon didn't say anything, he just raised an eyebrow.

"So then I said, 'Well, I don't go to dinner with guys who have wives *or* girlfriends,' and I walked away."

"Good answer."

"Anyway, I didn't see him again, and then the next Saturday, he showed up. And he told me that he had broken up with his girlfriend, and wanted to take me out. He was like, 'Well, things weren't going that great, and she wanted more than I was willing to give, and I didn't really want a ready-made family, yada yada yada.' And then he told me that he thought it was fate that we had met, and he couldn't stop thinking about me all week.

"The whole thing made me so uncomfortable, because I felt like maybe I was the reason he broke up with Ashley, and I hadn't done *anything* to encourage him, and I felt sorry for little Brooke if she had bonded with him, you know? So anyway, I told him I was busy and couldn't go out that night, and wasn't sure if I wanted to go out with him at all, and he just—well, Ryan's a salesman and he can be really persuasive. He ended up leaving that day, but he kept coming back almost every day, just being nice and real flirty, and he finally wore me down. So I went out with him, and it just—yeah, it just kept going."

"When did you get engaged?"

"Last July 4. We wanted a real simple wedding, and I'd always had my heart set on getting married in the fall, but his mother sort of took over and insisted that we needed more time to plan everything and make sure it was just right, so she picked New Year's Day."

"Why fall?" For some reason, Landon wanted to know.

Kelsea smiled. "It's my favorite season. I love the colors of fall."

He would file that away. "So, Ryan's mom picked your wedding date?"

I nodded. "I know, I should have run for the hills then. I just—well, I loved Ryan, and he always said things like, 'it's not the wedding that's important, it's the marriage,' and 'it's one day, we don't need to focus on that, we need to focus on spending the rest of our lives together.' He always defended her, said that it was just her way of showing her love. And he also went on and on about how she didn't have a daughter and would never get to plan a wedding."

"That wasn't *your* fault," Landon said. "For people that follow the tradition, the mothers with sons just don't get to plan a wedding."

Kelsea rubbed a hand over her eyes. "Anyway, it's over, and I'm so relieved that I won't have to put up with her for the next fifty years. But I think I still have doubts over how Ryan and I met. Right after we got engaged, I met someone who worked with Ashley, and she made me think that there was more to the story about hers and Ryan's break-up than he was telling me."

"Did you ever ask him about it?"

She nodded. "He always stuck to his original story. But now, I'm not so sure. I'm seeing more character flaws in him, and it wouldn't surprise me a bit if things weren't as they seemed."

Landon didn't say anything for a while. Then he asked,

"Do you still work at the zoo?" He wanted to hear her talk about her pet-sitting business.

"No, and I'm super sad about it. I loved every minute of it, and I think I would have been happy to stay there forever. But I'd been there about a year when my supervisor, a really nice gentleman named Rich who had worked at the zoo since just before I'd been born, called me into his office and gave me the bad news. Budget cutbacks. Deep cutbacks. He said he'd fought hard for me, but I didn't have seniority, and he had no choice."

"I'm sorry," Landon said.

"Thanks. No way was I going home to Mom with my tail between my legs. I like St. Louis—I live in one of the older suburbs, Kirkwood. So anyway, I took Sheldon and Penny to the dog park the next day, and I saw another dog mom there, Maggie, and we got to talking and I told her about being laid off, and told her I really wished I could get a job working with animals in some way. Then she had this great idea. They were going away for two weeks at the end of the month, and she said she'd rather pay me to take care of their dogs than board them. Do you have a dog?"

Landon shook his head. "I live in a condo in the city," he said. "Maybe someday."

"Well, you would not believe how much it was going to cost them to board their dogs. Maggie said she'd pay me the same amount, and then she paid me more to pick up their mail and keep an eye on the house. So I did that, and before I knew it, she helped me get other clients, and they referred me, and now I have a nice little business."

"Wow, that's impressive. Not everyone can run their own business."

"It works for me," she said. "And it's growing. If I get many more clients, I may need to think about hiring a part-time helper. I was thinking maybe a young teen. You know, they can't get a real job until they're sixteen, and it'd be nice to help one of them learn responsibility and earn some spending money."

Landon was impressed with her ingenuity and generous heart. "Sounds like a plan. Hey, I think you're starting to get a little pink," he said. "Where's the sunscreen?"

"Here," Kelsea said, handing it to him. She sat up and turned her away from him. "Would you get my back?"

With pleasure.

19

THE NEXT MORNING, Brandon and I ran again after breakfast, and then walked through some of the gardens around the resort. They were just beautiful, with gorgeous tropical flowers in more colors than I had ever seen in one place. The Queen's Garden, the destination for a special excursion on our last night on the island, was touted as the most spectacular garden on St. Jardin, and we agreed that we couldn't imagine anything being more beautiful than what we were seeing now.

After lunch, we decided to change into our suits and hit the beach. We swam for a while and then spread our towels on the pristine white sand.

I slathered sunscreen on and handed the bottle to Brandon. He knew without my having to ask that I wanted some rubbed on my back. I closed my eyes as his large, smooth hands went back and forth, up and down. *I could get used to this.*

When he stopped, I opened my eyes and he was putting sunscreen on himself. He handed the bottle to me and turned his back. I was happy to have an excuse to touch him.

What in the world are you thinking, Kelsea? You're hoping to get back with Ryan.

Then we both lay down on our stomachs. We chatted for a little while about inconsequential things, and then he went quiet. I turned my head one way, then the other, but couldn't relax. My mind kept going back to Brandon. The first time I saw him without a shirt, I nearly melted. I was really going to have to rethink my entire opinion about the male physique. Anyway, I couldn't believe that we'd spent the entire day together and hadn't fought once so far. *Maybe I'm losing my edge.*

I finally turned my head toward him, and opened my eyes. He had flipped onto his back. I took a moment to study at this man who both exasperated me and made me feel vibrant and alive. His hair was burnished gold from the sun, as were his eyebrows and long eyelashes. His nose marred what was otherwise a perfect, tanned face. I smiled as I recalled Brandon's story about breaking it in a hockey brawl. Actually, I think the crooked bump made him more attractive. I resisted the urge to sigh. He had a strong, defined jaw and a day's worth of growth that barely hid the deep cleft in his chin. I had the strongest desire to kiss it.

That left his lips. What would they feel like on mine? They looked firm but soft. Ever so slowly, I found myself leaning in a little closer, holding my breath.

Suddenly, his beautiful amber eyes popped open, and a slow smile spread across his face.

"Like what you see?" he said huskily.

I jumped back and quickly sat up. My heart pounded. "What are you talking about? I'm not looking at anything!" But my protests sounded lame, even to my ears.

"Hey, would you guys like to play volleyball?" I shielded my eyes from the sun and looked up to see Mark Wilder. *Saved by the ball.*

"Sounds fun!" I exclaimed, and popped up, brushing the sand from my legs.

Brandon raised up on his elbows. "I'm game."

Mark grinned. "You'll be on our team. Husbands against wives. Then we'll switch things up."

Brandon stood, and I boldly gave him a playful punch on his rock-hard stomach. *Oh, my.* "Did I tell you my nickname in high school was Spike?" I skipped away, ahead of them.

Brandon chased after me and caught me around my waist. "Don't forget, sweetheart, I've still got nine inches on you!"

I squealed with laughter. *Sweetheart.*

20

THE NEXT MORNING, their last day on St. Jardin began with a thunderstorm. Landon hoped he and Kelsea could get some private time inside today. He really needed to come clean with her about who he was, and maybe he'd even tell her that he lived in St. Louis.

Landon was so nervous that he nearly cut himself shaving, twice. He also went through three shirts before he changed back into the first one he'd had on. *Get a hold of yourself, man. This is ridiculous.*

He knocked on Kelsea's door. When she opened it, his breath caught. She looked bright and fresh and beautiful in white shorts, a cobalt blue top, and sandals. Her dark hair fell in damp waves past her shoulders.

"Hi," she smiled. "Wait, let me grab an umbrella—" She stopped when Landon held up his. "Oh, you've got one."

"Yep, I grabbed this one from my room."

They got to breakfast none the worse for wear due to huddling together under the umbrella between buildings. Kelsea let him pull her close as they ran through the rain, laughing and splashing. Landon had never done anything like that with Nicola.

They got their food and looked for a place to sit. Everyone seemed to have arrived at the same time this morning. "Are you thinking what I'm thinking?" she asked.

"Yeah, I am," Landon replied. "I've got the bird's eye view. Ah, there they are." They made a beeline for where Rose and Ike were sitting.

"Good morning, Brandon and Kelsea!" Rose called out. "It's good to see you. Isn't it a lovely day?"

Landon laughed. "It's raining, Rose."

"Yes, it is," Ike said. "But even the rainiest day on St. Jardin is better than the sunniest day in Brooklyn!"

Everyone laughed. "I agree, Ike," Kelsea said. "That goes for St. Louis, too."

"Besides, it'll move on, and we'll have a perfect day and more importantly, a perfect night for our closing festivities at the Queen's Garden," Rose said.

"Ooh, that sounds beautiful," Kelsea said.

"Is the Queen's Garden really the most extravagant one on the island?" Landon asked.

Rose and Ike nodded. "It is. There's no way to describe it," Rose exclaimed. "You have to see it to believe it."

"We were saying the other day that we couldn't imagine anything prettier than the gardens we've already seen," Kelsea commented.

"You're in for a real treat. We'll take everyone there by boat—it's on the other side of the island," Ike said. "Too far to walk, and our shuttle buses can't make it all the way there."

"Wear your walking shoes, Kelsea! You'll want to see

every bit of the garden. We'll get there in time to watch the sunset, and then we've got some special surprises in store for all of you."

Landon could hardly keep his eyes off Kelsea. He couldn't wait for tonight to arrive.

21

WE HAD BEEN instructed to dress for tonight, and for the women to wear white (but not a formal wedding dress), and comfortable shoes for walking. My dress was tea-length and strapless, with lace trim. I had a golden tan, and felt beautiful. I wore silver jewelry and high, glittering wedge sandals that were really quite comfortable.

When the knock came at the door, it startled me, even though I was expecting it. I adjusted my lace shawl and gave myself one last once-over in the mirror, smoothed my dress over my hips, grabbed my clutch, and walked to the door.

I let out a breath, and opened it.

I don't know what I was expecting, but it wasn't this.

Brandon's broad shoulders filled the doorway. He wore black pants and a white dinner jacket with a crisp white shirt and a black bow tie. His hair had lightened a little more with each day in the sun, and gleamed golden. Like me, he had a great tan.

Forget TDH. Now *this* was handsome.

He seemed a little tongue-tied, too. "Wow, you look

absolutely gorgeous," he said. His golden amber eyes glittered. He held out two red roses and a white one tied with a ribbon. "These are for you."

"I love roses!" I said appreciatively as I smelled them. "They're just beautiful."

"In the interest of full disclosure, they—Rose and Ike—provided these bouquets for everyone. But they were all a little different, and I chose these for you."

My heart did a little flip. "Thank you, Brandon."

"Kelsea, where's your ring?" he pointed to my left hand.

"Oh, I took it off before I got in the shower." I went over to the dresser and picked it up.

Brandon motioned to me. "Bring it here."

I walked over to him and laid it in his outstretched palm, and he slid the ring on my finger. As I watched, everything went into slow motion, like in a movie. It was a very intimate moment, and my stomach fluttered.

Had Ryan's hand ever felt like this on mine?

"There, all set," he said lightly. "Let's go."

He offered me his arm and we set off. I was so nervous. This felt like a date. Was I ready to move on? I didn't know a thing about Brandon, not about his family background, or what he did for a living, or even where he lived. What if this turned into something and I had to move thousands of miles away to be part of his life? I enjoyed my independence in St. Louis, but it was nice to be within a few hours' drive of my family.

I took a breath and was assaulted by his woodsy, masculine scent. It was perfect, just what a man should smell like. I snuck a glance at his profile. It was one thing to smell and look incredible, but he still got under my skin at times. I wasn't sure we were a good match at all. But I was getting way ahead of myself.

One part of me yearned to reunite with Ryan, because he was safe and secure. But that wasn't a given, and the other part kept telling me that I couldn't trust him. There were still too many unanswered questions. I knew that it would take me a long time to trust anyone again. And if and when I was ready for a new relationship, I wasn't at all sure that I would choose someone like Brandon. And to top it off, we were both on the rebound. Not the best recipe for long-term happiness.

Slow down, Kelsea, just slow down. I was ready to get home tomorrow, back to my tiny, manageable apartment, my dogs and my business and my life. I needed to get back in my routine, and wait for Ryan to come around.

But first, I had to get through tonight. Something told me that this was going to be a very special evening.

Brandon and I joined a line of other couples and followed them through the main garden toward the beach area. I could feel him standing behind me, and occasionally his body brushed against mine, sending little currents of electricity racing down my spine. At the dock stood a massive white yacht. Everyone chattered with excitement. The line slowed as we got closer to the ramp. When we got within sight of the entryway to the yacht, we discovered why.

Ike and Rose were standing at the top of the ramp, greeting everyone personally. Brandon gently rested his hands on my shoulders and leaned down to murmur in my ear, "Look at that, aren't they something?" I shivered involuntarily.

"They sure are." Ike was handsome in his tuxedo with a

pink shirt and tie, but it was Rose who was the belle of the ball. She wore a sparkling, pale pink tulle ball gown that glittered in the late afternoon sun, reminiscent of Glenda of the North in *Wizard of Oz*. Her bouffant hairdo was topped off by sparkling clips. As her hands waved around, more pink and white jewels reflected the light. I thought I caught a glimpse of her Converse.

"You know, theirs is the kind of marriage I'd like to have," Brandon mused. "I don't think I could have ever had that with Nicola." He gently squeezed my shoulders.

For a moment, I wondered what kind of marriage I might have had with Ryan, and might still have, if things worked out.

"Oh, Kelsea and Brandon!" Rose exclaimed when we reached her and Ike. She reached out and enfolded me in her arms. "You look beautiful, my dear! Just like a bride!" Ike and Brandon shook hands warmly.

I felt myself blushing. "Thank you, Rosie," I murmured.

Rose's arms fluttered around. "It's just perfect! You are the most beautiful woman here, isn't she, Brandon?" Rose stepped forward and reached up, wrapping her short arms around Brandon's waist as far as they could reach. He tenderly returned the hug, and I could tell that she and Ike had become very special to him.

They released one another, and Brandon gave both Rose and me an approving look. "I think it's a tie between you two ladies, Rose, but I'm honored to be Kelsea's escort tonight." He looked at both Rose and Ike. "Thank you both for everything. When I got here, my only goal was to survive the week." I felt his hand come lightly around my waist, and he looked down at me. "But it's been a great time instead."

"And it's not over yet!" Rose trilled, clapping her hands together.

"We'll see you later," I said, and we walked through the entrance onto the yacht.

A steward indicated where we should go. "Please, take the first empty spots you come to."

We sat, and Brandon rested his arm on the back of the seat. "This is a beautiful boat, isn't it? Have you ever been on anything like this?"

"Ah, no," I said. "What about you?"

He smiled. "No, nothing like this." I held my roses in my lap, and occasionally lifted them to my face. They were just heavenly. Before we knew it, we were underway. I felt like Brandon and I were alone, encapsulated in a lovely bubble, gliding through the water. His full attention was on me. It was like we were the only two people on the yacht.

I felt myself falling, and I was afraid he was falling with me.

22

KELSEA WAS FAR and away the most gorgeous woman here tonight, and she *did* look like a bride. The electricity hummed between them. Landon couldn't wait to get to the garden, where hopefully they could find a private spot to be alone for a few moments. There was so much he wanted to say to her. For one thing, he had to tell her his real name, and explain to her why he had deceived her and everyone else.

And Landon wanted to kiss her more than he'd ever wanted to kiss any woman in his entire life.

But for now, sitting close to her was enough. Deep down, he sensed that she was skittish, and didn't want to scare her off with the intensity of what he was feeling.

The trip around the perimeter of the island took less time than he thought it would. Landon felt the purring engines cut back, and soon they went completely silent, and the crew guided the yacht next to a large dock and began to tie up.

Everyone was murmuring about the scenery. This side of the island appeared to be somewhat rockier. The cliff that faced the water sloped sharply upward, and there were two symmetrical staircases winding up in gentle curves. On both sides, foliage in myriad hues of green covered the slopes with brightly colored flowers interspersed throughout. It was simply enchanting.

As they pulled up to the dock, Rose's voice came over the PA system. "Yoo hoo, brides and grooms!" Everyone laughed. "Welcome to the Queen's Garden, the most splendid spot on all of St. Jardin. When you exit the yacht, you may ascend by either staircase. Ladies, I hope you brought your Converse!" More laughter. "Hold on tight to the handrails, and gentlemen, hold on to your woman!" That brought the loudest laughter of all.

"When we arrive at the garden, there will be hors d'oeuvres and champagne, fruit punch, and sparkling water, and then a dinner buffet when we return to the resort. You may go anywhere in the garden, except the Majestic Meadow at the far south end, which is being prepared for the finale later this evening. The entrance to that will be roped off. There are benches everywhere that you may sit on. And I'm sorry, but the government of St. Jardin does not allow photography of any kind in the garden." Murmurs of disappointment rippled through the crowd.

"It is our national treasure, and most areas are considered sacred ground and are not permitted to be photographed. When we return to the resort, there will be photographs that you may purchase."

"Now, let's synchronize our watches. It's exactly 5:30. You will have ninety minutes to enjoy the garden, and promptly at 7:00, we will assemble at the entrance to the Majestic Meadow. Welcome to the Queen's Garden!" she concluded with a flourish.

Landon and Kelsea filed off with the others, and when they reached the staircase, she placed her elegant hand on the black filigree railing and began to climb. He was happy to follow her and enjoy the view—and not just of the flora and fauna, either.

When they reached the top, the garden stretched out before them. There really were no words. Landon looked down at Kelsea, and her hand flew up to her cheek. He heard soft gasps from many of the others.

"Can you believe this?" she exclaimed. I've never seen so many shades of green in my life! And the flowers!"

Landon could hardly form a coherent thought. He was certain that this was the Garden of Eden come to life. They would have to descend more stairs to reach the meadow—probably half the number that they had just climbed. As far as the eye could see in front of them were flowers of every color of the rainbow, trees of every kind imaginable—even flowering trees in pinks and purples—and cobblestone paths winding through the lush grass. Far beyond the tallest trees at the opposite end of the garden were sloping, tree-covered blue-green hills. The sky above them was a deep sapphire, dotted with white clouds.

Gazing upon this amazing beauty was almost a spiritual experience. Landon wanted so badly to be connected to Kelsea during this moment, and held out his hand. He wanted to make the offer and let her decide.

When she slid her fingers through his, Landon knew that this was, without a doubt, the most perfect moment of his life. Without speaking, they started down the staircase. When they reached the garden, they kept walking. It seemed that every flower in existence was there. Landon thought the tulips were the most beautiful he'd ever seen. The rose-covered arbor was Kelsea's favorite.

There were areas dripping with moss, waterfalls, and ponds with lily pads, with a shooting fountain in the middle of one of them. Every time Landon thought he'd seen the most beautiful thing ever, something else topped it around the next corner.

One of the best things about sharing this experience with Kelsea was that they hardly spoke. It was almost like being in one of the cathedrals of Europe, where it was sacrilegious to speak. But Landon felt that they were communicating in ways that went beyond words.

When they returned to the main garden, they got a few things to eat, and cups of fruit punch. Kelsea was glowing. "Are you enjoying yourself?" Landon asked her.

She nodded, her eyes alight with wonder. "I could never have imagined this place! Doesn't it remind you of the Garden of Eden from the Bible?"

Landon grinned at her. "That was the first thing that came into my mind when we saw it for the first time." They walked together on the path up to a little rise that somehow they had missed before.

Suddenly, she grabbed his arm. "Brandon, look!"

He followed her finger, which pointed out toward the way from they'd originally come, up the stairs from the yacht and then down into the garden. Beyond the top of the stairs, they could see clear out to the view of the turquoise sea. It was beyond breathtaking.

"I feel completely at peace," Kelsea said quietly as she stared toward the incredible view. "Rose said that the beauty of the island would restore my soul, and she was right. I don't know what will happen when I get home, but I know God has a plan, and there was a reason all of this happened." She looked at Brandon. "I don't know whether Ryan and I will get back together, but I can accept whatever happens."

Landon was relieved to discover that they were alone on the rise. It was the perfect place and time. "Kelsea, there's something I need to tell you," he said, and took both of her hands in his.

"Attention, brides and grooms!" Rose's voice blasted out through a speaker system loud and clear. "It's time to line up for the procession to the Royal Marriage Ceremony."

Royal Marriage Ceremony? Landon had a hard time concentrating on the rest of what Rose was saying, his heart was pounding so hard. Kelsea withdrew her hands from his.

"This ceremony has been a custom on St. Jardin for over eight hundred years. It is a beautiful ritual with a symbolic connection to nature and the universe, but it is not legally binding, since none of you are citizens of St. Jardin."

Landon relaxed, but couldn't bring himself to look at Kelsea.

"Please proceed to the entrance to the Majestic Meadow and line up, brides on the right, grooms on the left. Stay with your partner until you reach the Grand Rose Bower. Grooms will file in first, and line up in a large semi-circle in the meadow. Then the brides will follow and stand facing their groom. Brides, I hope you still have your small bouquets. Everyone, stay in your place in line so you will end up with the right partner when you reunite in the Meadow!" There was laughter all around, but Landon wasn't laughing.

He positioned himself on Kelsea's left and they walked to the south end of the garden with the other couples. The line stopped, and they waited. Landon had no idea what to expect. *Maybe we can get out of this.*

23

I COULD HARDLY believe my ears as I listened to Rose's instructions. Even though she said it wasn't legal, it seemed that Brandon and I were going to have to participate in some kind of ritualistic marriage ceremony. I felt a growing connection between us, but this made me uncomfortable.

When the line stopped, we just stood there. I had a hyperawareness of Brandon right next to me, but I was afraid to look at him. What was he thinking?

Soon, I heard Rose's voice coming closer and, sure enough, she was parading down the line on the brides' side in her Converse, holding her skirt up with both hands. As soon as I saw her, I waved as inconspicuously as I could. Her eyes lit up when she saw me.

"Kelsea and Brandon!" she said when she reached us. I grabbed on to her hands.

"Rosie, I—um—" *Oh, this was awkward.*

I steeled myself and glanced up at Brandon. Right away, I knew that he was feeling exactly as I was. I swear he sent me a telepathic message. *I like where we're headed, but I'm not ready for this.*

"Ah, Rose," Brandon said. He looked at me, and I tried to message him back. *Please, let her down gently.* "We aren't really, that is—could we just sit on one of the benches—"

"Oh, no, that wouldn't do at all. This is a very sacred ceremony, and it would offend the native St. Jardinians who have worked so hard to prepare this for us." Rose squeezed my hands. "You two are going to be just fine. I promise, once you've experienced this, you'll be so happy that you did."

She let go of my hands and moved on.

Brandon leaned down and said in a stage whisper, "Did you ever do theatre or drama in high school?"

"No," I said, shaking my head.

"Me, neither," he said. "I was going to say something about just pretending like we were in a school play."

Despite my nervousness, I giggled. "Oh, gosh, how did we end up here?"

Brandon nudged my arm with his. "We came in a boat!" Then we both started laughing.

The grooms' line began to move forward. "Well, here we go," he said. "See ya!" He smiled and gave me a little wave as he walked away.

I was probably the only "bride" that was nervous at the prospect of this ceremony. Really, the source of my unease was due to only one unanswered question.

Whether Brandon and I would be expected to kiss at the conclusion of the ceremony.

24

LANDON BENT DOWN for a native woman to drape a long, colorful lei around his neck, then filed through a fragrant archway of red and white roses.

When he stepped into the Majestic Meadow, he felt like he was in a cathedral, on holy ground. The meadow stretched out before them, sloping downward, a carpet of pristine, green grass. On the other side was a backdrop of trees and flowers and just in front of them, a sparkling, clear stream running the entire width of the meadow.

A group of men and women in native costume were gathered at one end of the meadow, playing drums, hand-held percussion instruments, and several instruments of various sizes that Landon thought might be ukuleles. A sweet melody danced on the air, unlike anything he had ever heard.

The sun was just beginning to set, but the meadow was awash in firelight, the result of one hundred tall torches set in a perfect semi-circle. As the men quietly filed in, they were instructed by one of the ceremonial participants to stand in front of the next torch when the line stopped.

All of Landon's reservations about the ceremony evaporated, and were replaced by a feeling of peace. The incredible sights, sounds, and aromas floated around him, and somehow, he knew God was here, and that everything was going to be all right.

He didn't know how long they stood there, but suddenly he realized that the music had stopped. About ten seconds later, he heard the faint tinkling of bells, which grew louder as the brides entered, and he realized that each woman was holding a small set of metal chimes. Then some flute-like instruments began to play, and finally, all the brides had arrived.

Kelsea faced him, and Landon knew he had never seen a more beautiful woman. She was a vision of loveliness in the white, lacy dress, and wore a crown of flowers that matched the ones around his neck. There was a serenity surrounding her that Landon was sure he hadn't seen in the week that they'd been on the island.

A male voice came over the PA system. "Brides, please turn around and stand directly in front of your groom." All two hundred participants were now facing the same direction, looking out over the stream to the backdrop of tall trees. The meadow was so vast, even a crowd of that size felt dwarfed. And as Landon laid his hands on Kelsea's waist, he felt like they were the only two people there.

Three men dressed in elegant, traditional costumes stood before them on a raised rock dais, visible to everyone. One stood in the center, higher than the other two, and Landon assumed he was the priest. His costume was more extravagant than the others. He began to speak in French, and the two men on either side of him translated in both English and Spanish.

The symbol of love is the beauty of nature, the English translator said. Landon leaned forward and clasped Kelsea's arms lightly, and she rested her head on his chest.

The ceremony continued with prayers and beautiful native dances by the musicians. Then, the brides were directed to turn and face their grooms, lay their bouquets down, and everyone was asked to remove their shoes, and in the case of the men, their socks. When Landon's bare feet touched the grass, he swore it was the softest he had ever felt.

The priest asked for brides and grooms to clasp hands. "You wear matching leis and crowns," he said, "to symbolize harmony. The seven flowers that comprise them represent seven aspects of marriage: friendship, fertility, passion, loyalty, faithfulness, partnership, and everlasting love." As he heard the words of the translator, Landon relished the feel of Kelsea's soft, feminine hands in his, and was surprised that it wasn't awkward for either of them to look into one another's eyes.

When the priest finished the litany, the musicians broke into a lyrical, mesmerizing song and dance, this one with flowing ribbons. Following its conclusion, women dressed in a different kind of native costume circulated among the couples, offering everyone plastic flutes of crystal-clear water. When everyone had been served, the priest spoke.

"You now hold in your hand, water from the Fountain of Marital Bliss. Link arms with your partner, and drink deeply from the cup that they hold." Landon held Kelsea's gaze in his as they drank.

"This water now flows through your body and will saturate every cell. You are bound for life. What God has joined together, let nothing separate. I now pronounce you husband and wife."

The priest smiled. "Now, as I'm sure you have all been anticipating, we will conclude with a western custom, the bridal kiss, with an added piece of St. Jardinian folklore." Laughter rippled through the crowd.

"Husbands, draw your wife to you, and loop your lei around her neck, so that it surrounds both of you, representing that the two of you are one. Then, wives, step up onto your husband's feet. It will be necessary for you to work together, to hold on to one another to stay balanced, symbolic of how you should approach every step of your marriage journey. Husbands, you may now kiss your wife."

Landon thought his heart might stop. He drew Kelsea close as she stepped up onto his feet. She fit perfectly in his arms. Where Nicola was sharp angles, Kelsea was soft curves, and filled all the empty spaces of his heart. Her dark brown eyes glowed in the waning twilight and firelight, and she looked like a woman who deeply desired to be kissed.

Still, he wanted to be sure. "May I kiss you now?" he whispered for her ears only.

Without hesitation, Kelsea nodded, and Landon lowered his lips to hers.

25

DEEP DOWN, I knew a kiss would be part of the ceremony and that I would have to endure it, but when the time came, it was something I wanted, not an obligation. I felt covered by a cloak of serenity and peace. Everything about this ceremony made me want to be connected to the man whose feet I stood on, whose strong arms were around me.

When Brandon's lips touched mine, I melted clear down to the tips of my fingers and toes. The world around me ceased to exist, and all I cared about was being with him. He held me tightly, but I didn't feel trapped in any way.

This was, without a doubt, the softest, sweetest, most sensual kiss of my life. It was a long kiss, but there was no urgency about it, and I sensed that Brandon felt that he could go on kissing me like this forever. I could, too.

When we finally pulled apart, he rested his forehead on mine. "Wow," he whispered.

A soft giggle escaped. "Yes, wow," I whispered back.

He looked at me, his expression solemn. "There's so much I want to say to you, Kelsea, but right now, I just need to hold you."

I didn't hesitate, and wrapped my arms around him, resting my head on his shoulder, breathing him in.

Rose's voice over the PA system brought us back to reality. "Congratulations, everyone! We hope you enjoyed this most special display of St. Jardinian tradition and culture. Would you please thank our hosts with a round of applause?"

I stepped out of Brandon's embrace and we both clapped heartily along with everyone else. When it died down, Rose spoke again. "You may put your shoes on now, and return through the garden to the staircases that will take you back to the yacht. Please proceed as quickly as possible. We have one more surprise for you after we board!"

We donned our shoes, and I picked up my bouquet. Brandon took my hand and we walked silently to the yacht. There was little talk on anyone's part. I think we all were still under the spell of the touching ceremony.

When we found our seats, Brandon slipped his arm around my shoulders, and I snuggled into him. The boat's engines started up, and we pulled away from the island. Suddenly, to everyone's surprise and delight, the sky before us lit up with an explosion of fireworks.

It was the perfect end to a perfect evening.

26

LANDON FELT LIKE he was in some kind of parallel universe, and never wanted it to end. As the yacht slid away from the island, the spectacular fireworks display got smaller and smaller in the distance. He knew that couples all around them were kissing, and he wanted nothing more than to join them. Only one thing held him back.

He was afraid that if he kissed Kelsea again, that he wouldn't be able to stop.

His heart beat an erratic rhythm. Rose was right. Landon *was* glad that they participated in the ceremony. He couldn't imagine having gone through it with Nicola, but couldn't put his finger on the reason why.

Now, all he could think about was how he and Kelsea would move forward from here. He thought the beautiful wedding ceremony was a great foundation from which to begin. But first and foremost, he *had* to tell her who he was, and more importantly, that he lived and worked so close to her in St. Louis. Landon imagined her ecstatic reaction to hearing that news. He also needed to be truthful with her about how he knew what her former fiancé had been up to, and that he'd put an investigator on the case to dig up all the dirt on Ryan.

Kelsea scooted a little closer to him, and he tightened his hold on her. His heart took wing as he thought of holding her like this for many years to come. He loved that they could just sit like this without having to talk.

It had been just one week since he was left at the altar, and now he had a future with a woman whom he already loved in a way that he'd never loved Nicola. Landon's heart was filled with gratitude.

The yacht arrived back at the resort, and they filed off with the other guests. Landon smiled down at Kelsea and took her hand, and her answering smile made his heart swell.

"Do you want to go to the buffet?" he asked quietly. He wasn't sure he could eat anything, his stomach was so jumpy.

She tucked a strand of dark hair behind one ear. "I'm not really hungry," she said, "but I didn't eat much at the garden, so I should probably get something."

Landon didn't think he could eat anything either, but changed his mind when they arrived in the main dining hall and the delicious scents of the buffet enveloped them. They filled their plates and sat with three other couples and made small talk about the incredible Queen's Garden.

The others left, and Kelsea and Landon started the walk back to their rooms. He didn't want things to get awkward. "Would you like to take one last walk on the beach?"

Kelsea's eyes lit up. "I'd love it! Who needs to sleep? I can sleep tomorrow night when the tropical breezes and sounds of the sea are just a memory."

They stopped at her door. "I'll change and be right back," he said.

"I'll be waiting," she replied with a smile.

Landon quickly changed and freshened up. As he looked in the mirror, he wondered if Kelsea would be in his arms when the sun came up. He fully intended to tell her tonight that he was in love with her, but had no idea where it would go from there. *I'd appreciate a little help here, God,* he prayed.

27

I WAS SO relieved when Brandon suggested a walk on the beach. I didn't want to arrive in our hallway and have some awkward conversation about what would come next. I had almost decided to invite him to my room, but didn't want to send the wrong message. I couldn't believe we would be going our separate ways in the morning, and wanted to spend every moment of this last night with him, just talking and looking into his gorgeous dark amber eyes, and hopefully be on the receiving end of a few more of his bone-melting kisses.

The problem with that is that with very little encouragement, I was sure it could lead to a lot more, and I didn't know if I was ready to take that step. I wasn't a virgin, but it had been about a decade since I'd made the decision to wait for marriage, and I still believed that was right for me.

I quickly brushed my teeth and started to brush the tangles out of my hair. My heart skipped a beat when a knock came at the door. I opened it, hairbrush in hand. Landon wore his University of Minnesota hoodie with the flowered lei from the ceremony. The combination of those two items made me giggle.

"Come on in. I'm just putting my hair up." I didn't want to have to fight with it in the seaside wind. I didn't want anything to distract me from being with Brandon. Maybe he would finally tell me where he was from and more about himself. If he was from Minnesota, maybe he lived in the Midwest. Maybe it wouldn't be so bad, if we decided to move forward together. I looked at the harried woman in the mirror. *One step at a time, Kelsea.*

When I came out of the bathroom, he was standing just where I'd left him. "You're so beautiful," he said as I approached. I felt heat rise to my cheeks. I was wearing shorts and a hoodie, hardly the definition of *beautiful*.

"Thank you." He took my hands and we just stood there, smiling at one another. Then he looped the lei around my neck, and I took a step closer.

"Could I—" Brandon closed his eyes for a second and took a breath. Then he opened them and exhaled loudly. "Could I please kiss you again?"

He's adorable when he's nervous. I laid my hands on his shoulders. "You don't have to ask," I said softly. His hands came securely around my waist, and his heart-stopping grin made my stomach flip.

Just as Brandon lowered his head, a loud knock on the door made us jump apart. Brandon lifted the lei off of both of us. *Of all the lousy timing.* My heart pounded as I opened the door to one of the resort's employees holding a large floral bouquet.

"Kelsea Anderson?"

"Yes, that's me."

"These were delivered for you while you were gone."

"Thank you." I took the vase, and closed the door. I smiled at Brandon. "These are beautiful! Are you responsible?"

"I wish I could take credit, but they're not from me. Maybe Ike and Rose sent them to all the brides."

"If they wanted to do that, they could have left them in our rooms while we were away. He said they were delivered for me. No one knows that I'm here."

"No one?" Brandon echoed.

"Just Morgan," I replied.

I set the vase down, tore open the envelope, and read the card.

My heart pounded. I looked up at Brandon. I read the card again to make sure that I wasn't dreaming. "They're from Ryan," I whispered, in shock.

He frowned. "How did he know you were here?"

"He must have called Morgan." I held the card out to him.

"You want me to read it?" Brandon asked. I nodded.

He read out loud the words that were already engraved on my heart. *"Dear Kels, I know I screwed up bad. I want to try to make this work. Counting the minutes until you come home. Love, Ryan."*

I fingered the petals of the beautiful flowers and bent to inhale their delicious scent. "He wants me back! He still loves me!"

I began dancing around the room and, next thing I knew, I had thrown my arms exuberantly around Brandon. "Oh, Brandon, I was right! He just needed some space! It's all going to work out!" I untangled myself from him and sat down on the couch.

I pressed my hands to my cheeks to find that they were wet with tears of joy. "I knew he would come around."

"Kelsea."

I released a pent-up breath. "He just needed some time."

"Kelsea." This time Brandon's voice was a little louder, a little firmer.

"What?" I stopped and looked at him. His arms hung limply at his side. "Brandon, what's wrong? Aren't you happy for me?"

He rubbed a hand over his jaw.

"I guess I'm just—after what we shared at the Queen's Garden, and everything—I thought—"

My heart began to pound. *Oh, no.* "Brandon, it was—special. Really, I've learned a lot from you this week. But I've invested almost *three years* of my life with Ryan. If there was a chance of making it work with Nicola again, wouldn't you jump at it?" Then I saw the look on his face, and realized how insensitive I'd been. "Brandon, I'm sorry—"

"I'm sorry, too," he said, his voice clipped. He rested his hands on his hips, and a tic worked in his jaw. "What would have happened if that delivery person hadn't knocked on the door just now?"

"I, I don't know," I whispered. I looked down at my hands for several silent seconds. Then I removed the beautiful tri-gold band and held it out. "Maybe you should take this back now."

"Kelsea—" He looked at me for a long moment, his expression unreadable. Finally, he reached out and took the ring, and put it in his pocket. "You need to be open to the possibility that things with Ryan may not be what they seem."

"What do you mean? It couldn't be any clearer." I held the note up.

"I just—I just don't want you to get hurt."

He wasn't making any sense. "How can I get hurt? Ryan *loves* me! He wants to make it work!" I scowled at him and crossed my arms in front of me. "Why can't you be happy for me? I'd be happy for you if the tables were turned."

Brandon hesitated, then came and sat down next to me. "Get your computer. I need to show you something."

I didn't move. "Why? What are you talking about?"

"Just go to Ryan's social media page."

This made no sense at all. "What are you talking about? Why would you care about Ryan's page? He hardly ever goes on there." Really, I was beginning to get annoyed.

But the look on his face made me think again. I got my computer, signed on, then navigated to Ryan's page. I scanned it, but didn't see anything. It looked like he hadn't updated anything in a while. No surprise there.

"What? What am I looking for, Brandon?"

"Right there—" he pointed, then dropped his hand. "It was there, but now it's gone."

"What was there?"

"There"—he pointed again—"it used to say *in a relationship with Jenna Harmon.*"

I looked at the screen. *No relationship info to show.* "What are you talking about? Who's Jenna Harmon? And what were you doing on Ryan's page, anyway?"

"I came on his page the first night we were here, after you told me his name, and it was right there in black and white." His expression turned serious. "Kelsea, there's more."

I slammed my computer shut and jumped up. "I don't believe you! And you had no business stalking him, anyway! What in the world is wrong with you, Brandon? Do you hate me so much that you'd try to ruin my chance to get back with the man I love?"

He stood. "Kelsea, I had an investigator look into it—"

I was horrified. "You what?" I shouted. "This was none of your business!" I was seriously starting to get creeped out. Who was Brandon St. Fair, anyway? What if he reached out to Ryan and told him that he'd met me this week, and that we'd pretended to be married, and even kissed? I knew nothing about Brandon, and yet, somehow this week, in my weakened emotional state, I'd fallen under his spell.

My heart pounded. What if that delivery person *hadn't* interrupted us? My mind began to go in all kinds of wild directions.

"Kelsea, let me explain—"

I needed time to think. "Get out!" I screamed. Tears coursed down my cheeks. "Please, just go. I have to think."

"You're making a mistake, Kelsea. Let me help you."

"Get. Out. NOW!"

Brandon walked to the door and opened it. Then he turned and looked at me.

"OUT!"

He closed the door quietly behind him.

28

LANDON WENT BACK to his room and paced. He felt like a caged animal, and decided to go for a run on the beach, *alone*.

That lying weasel, Ryan Singer. He must have taken Jenna Harmon's name off his page for some reason, maybe when he decided that he wanted to try to make up with Kelsea. Landon's stomach churned. She deserved so much better than this guy. Singer had bigger problems, and Landon desperately wanted Kelsea to be spared from all of it.

Landon couldn't tell her that after first seeing Ryan's page, he'd made a call to one of his firm's investigators and asked him to do a little more poking around. Ben Nelson was a young, tech-savvy guy, and this was right up his alley. It was all over social media, thanks to Jenna Harmon. And thanks to her young friends sharing every moment of their lives online, Ben was easily able to catch up with them at their favorite bar, pose as a co-worker of Jenna and Ryan, and get all the sordid details of their fling.

It was much worse than Landon could have imagined.

When Ben had called and filled him in, Landon was relieved that Kelsea was free of Singer. But now it was all going to blow up in her face.

Landon ran hard, reveling in the feeling of pushing his body to its physical limits. His heart pounded, and the endorphins flowed as his long legs pounded along the sand. He ran to banish the memories of the entire evening at the Queen's Garden.

But as long as Landon lived, he knew he would never forget that kiss, and every other detail about the most magical evening of his life.

He ran like he was being chased by the devil, and he knew what he was really trying to run from. Finally, he finished, exhausted, then cooled down and walked up from the beach and through the garden to the main building.

He needed to talk with Rose and Ike.

29

I WAS LIVID. Brandon St. Fair was the lowest human being on the planet, and I wouldn't spend one more second in his presence. Not one more! Thanks goodness I was leaving first thing in the morning. I didn't even want to be in the same hemisphere as him.

The nerve of him, making up some story about Ryan being in a relationship with some non-existent person named Jenna. What was he trying to prove, anyway? That I had to stay jilted just because he was? I meant what I'd said, that I'd be happy for him if Nicola had taken him back.

But then I thought of the magical time at the Queen's Garden, of the moving ceremony, and of that incredible kiss. It seemed like weeks ago instead of hours. As soon as I read Ryan's words, everything changed. And now I was so confused.

I spent some time packing so I wouldn't have to do anything in the morning. Then I sat down with my computer and looked at Ryan's page. I started clicking, and then had another idea. What if there was another Ryan Singer in St.

Louis, and Brandon had just been on the wrong page? I could settle this, once and for all. I typed *Jenna Harmon St. Louis* into the search engine and held my breath. There were two entries. I clicked on the first. This Jenna was at least 40 years old, was married, and had three kids and a Dalmatian. *Whew.*

I clicked on the second one, and my heart stopped. This Jenna was in her mid-20s, with long, luxurious blonde curls and big, expertly made-up blue eyes. This Jenna worked for the same company as Ryan. And this Jenna was *in a relationship with Ryan Singer.*

I pressed my hand over my mouth. *Okay, maybe it's another Ryan Singer.* So I did a little searching and found a headshot of her and Ryan nestled together.

My jaw dropped. It was definitely *my* Ryan. It looked like they were in a bar. They were both smiling and honestly, they looked a little drunk. The date listed was the night before Thanksgiving. I'd gone home to my Mom's to spend one last holiday with her and Morgan, just the three of us. Ryan insisted he'd be fine without me. He said he'd have dinner with his mom and use the time to get ahead on some of his work in preparation for being gone for our honeymoon.

But it was obvious he had found other ways to occupy himself in my absence. I hadn't seen him for a few days after I returned. He said he was getting over the flu.

There were no more pictures of Ryan and Jenna. I kept scrolling and stopped at a post that was dated the day Ryan broke up with me. My stomach heaved. There was a selfie of an ecstatic Jenna holding one of those home pregnancy test wands. *Best way to begin the new year! I'M PREGNANT!* the caption screamed.

30

LANDON WALKED INTO the dining hall, where the buffet was just winding down. His eyes scanned the room and to his immense relief, he saw Rose and Ike.

"Brandon! Or can we call you Landon now?" Rose said. "What did you and Kelsea think of the ceremony?"

Landon sat and tried to dredge up a smile. "Ah, we enjoyed it very much. It really was an incredible experience."

"But something's happened." Rose and Ike both looked at him with concern.

"Kelsea received some news from home. It's complicated." He looked down at his hands, at the ring on his finger, and felt sadness. He looked at Rose. "She could use a friend tonight, if you could check in on her."

Rose's gaze speared right through him. "Seems that you two have become pretty good friends, *Mr. St. Clair.*"

Landon winced, then nodded. "We have, but there was never a good time for me to tell her why I lied about my name. And now, it would—" He rubbed a hand over his face.

"It just wouldn't work. She's not speaking to me right now, and she's planning to go back to her fiancé."

"Is this news from home about him?" Rose asked.

"Yes, yes it is. But there's more to the story than she knows, and she may figure it out soon. If not, I think I have to tell her. And it's just going to kill her." Landon looked down and was surprised to see that he was twisting the wedding band around on his finger.

Rose and Ike exchanged a look. "It seems that when she gets more bad news, she'll need more than a friend to turn to," Rose said. "She'll need someone who loves her."

Landon went completely still, his head still down. When he finally lifted it, he met Rose and Ike's tender gazes. "It's nothing to be ashamed of, son," Ike said softly.

"I'm not ashamed," Landon said, "it's just bad timing, I guess. She's still in love with Singer."

"She *thinks* she's in love with him," Rose corrected. "Remember, she's known him a lot longer than she's known you. When anyone has emotional upheaval in their life, they grab on to anything familiar and comfortable. The only thing you can do right now is wait for her, and be there when she gets to the bottom of everything and realizes that she's in love with *you.*"

Landon shook his head. "She's not in love with me," he said.

Rose and Ike smiled at one another. "She is," Rose said emphatically. "She's just not ready to admit it yet."

Ike reached for Rose's hand. "Sounds like another beautiful young lady I knew once," he said with a smile. Then he looked at Landon and raised an eyebrow.

"Really?" Landon looked between the two.

Rose sighed. "Oh, yes. It took me a long time to come around. My Ike was the soul of patience."

"From the time I fell in love with her, I waited for ten months," Ike proclaimed.

Landon rubbed a hand through his hair. "I've only known Kelsea for six days. And exactly a week ago, I was fully prepared to marry someone else."

"That was my situation when I met Ike," Rose said. "I'd been dating this dashing Irishman—really, it was a whirlwind courtship—and he had promised to marry me and take me back to Ireland with him. But then he was arrested for being part of a theft ring, and off to prison he went."

"Were you still carrying a torch for him?" Landon asked.

"Was I ever! I told myself that I would wait for him no matter how long it took."

"My family owned a deli and market in Rose's neighborhood," Ike said. "I worked there, and she came in quite a bit and really caught my eye, but I was too shy to speak up."

"He was quiet as a mouse," Rose said. "My brother George was a beat cop, and knew the Goldmans well."

"We always gave the cops free coffee and pastries," Ike said with a smile. "George was a friendly sort, and I finally got up the nerve to ask him about his sister. He told me that she had been planning to marry someone, but the guy went to jail, and was going to be deported back to Ireland to stand trial there."

Rose shuddered. "It turns out he and his gang had fled to New York from Ireland after a botched robbery there that resulted in the deaths of two men," Rose said. "So anyway,

I was just moping around, and I was only eighteen, and I was *sure* that he would write to me and send passage, and then I would go to Ireland and marry him and visit him in prison. I was so naïve. After about six months, I still hadn't heard a word from him, and George had finally had it with my sackcloth-and-ashes routine, and told me that I should let Ike Goldman court me. My response was, 'Ike Goldman? Who in the world is Ike Goldman?'"

They both laughed, and Landon laughed with them.

"I'd made no impression whatsoever on her!" Ike said. "I was just plodding along, trying to work up the courage to say hello to her, and lo and behold, one day she came into the store with George and he introduced us, and she suggested that we go for a walk the next afternoon."

Landon smiled. "Once you figured out who Ike was, you must have liked what you saw," he said to Rose.

"I did, but I was still carrying a torch for Tommy O'Houlihan," Rose sighed. "I wasn't interested in anything but friendship with Ike, but he stuck with me and I finally came around."

Landon looked at Ike. "Was there ever a time that you doubted her? Did you think the two of you might not ever get together?"

Ike shook his head. "I knew deep in my soul that this was the woman God chose for me." He squeezed Rose's hand. "And I was willing to wait as long as it took. Just having her friendship was more than I'd had. I was happy enough for that."

Landon shook his head. "I admire your patience, Ike. I feel like I've been through a hurricane. But I know that I love Kelsea, and I'll wait as long as it takes."

Rose patted his hand. "She'll come around, I'm sure of it."

"Well, I know she won't open the door to me tonight," Landon said. "So would you be willing to check in on her?"

"We'll do better than that," Rose replied. She picked up the two-way radio sitting on the table next to her. "Front desk, we need an extra key card for Miss Anderson's room. Mr. St. Fair will come by to pick that up in a few minutes."

"Yes, Ma'am," came the reply.

Landon rested his hands on his knees. "I'm not sure that's a good idea."

Rose smiled. "It is. Trust us."

Ike stared at Landon, his gaze steady. "You can't leave her like this."

Landon looked at them for a long moment.

"You're right. Thanks, both of you. I can't thank you enough." He smiled. "If we get through this in one piece, we'll name our first son and daughter after you."

He was happy that this elicited a hearty laugh from the couple. He stood and squeezed their hands. "We'll be praying for you, son," Ike said.

When was the last time anyone had prayed for him? The thought lightened his footsteps.

Landon got the key card from the front desk and went straight to Kelsea's room. He took a deep breath, then knocked.

"Kelsea, it's me. Please, can we talk?"

No answer.

He knocked again, a little louder. He didn't want to roust any of the neighbors, but it was important to make it clear to her what he intended to do. "Kelsea, if you're there, please open the door. I just want to make sure you're okay."

Landon stood there in silence, willing his breathing to slow down. It was possible that she'd gone out on a walk, but he felt deep in his bones that she was in the room.

He took a cleansing breath. "Kelsea, Rose gave me a key card. I'm coming in now." He swiped the card and slowly opened the door.

The room was dark except for one of the bedside lamps. Landon saw water reflected on the floor, broken shards of glass everywhere, and crushed, wilted flowers.

Kelsea sat in a corner of the sofa, rolled up in a ball. Rumpled tissues littered the area around her, and her laptop was open on the table. Landon stepped closer and glanced at the screen. He wasn't at all surprised at what he saw.

Slowly, he lowered himself down and sat next to her, leaving some space between them. Neither of them said anything, and Kelsea seemed to be staring at some faraway spot. After several minutes, Landon began to grow concerned that she was in some kind of catatonic state or something.

"How did you know?" She finally said in a low voice. She still wouldn't look at him.

Oh, this was going to be sticky. "Well, um, I—that first night after you told me Ryan's name, I went on his social media page."

"You stalked him." She crossed her arms in front of her chest and continued to stare straight ahead.

"I was just—curious. And that night, on his page, it said that he was in a relationship with Jenna Harmon. So then, I went to *her* page, and it said that she was in a relationship with someone else, not Ryan."

"*Not* Ryan?"

"Correct." Now came the hard part, and due to Kelsea's state of mind, Landon didn't feel that this was the right moment to reveal that he had lied about his identity. This was a mine field, and he had to step carefully. "So. I'm—in my line of work, I use the services of private investigators, so I contacted one of them and asked him to poke around a little. And he reported back to me about the pregnancy."

Kelsea jumped up and began to pace. "So then, you thought you would just flirt with me, spend time together, get me into your good graces, get me to go along with some fake wedding ceremony, and then sleep with me."

Landon leapt to his feet. "Are you kidding me, Kelsea? How could I have had any idea about the ceremony tonight? None of us knew anything about that."

She came and stood right in front of him. "Empty your pockets, Brandon," she ordered.

"What? What are you talking about?"

"Empty your pockets, now." Her eyes flashed at him.

"I don't know what you're looking for, but here you go." He took out his key card and slapped it down on the table. He pulled the linings of both of shorts pockets out, stretched his front hoodie pocket out, and stuck his hand through it so she could see that it was empty.

"No cell phone?"

"I didn't want any distractions."

"No wallet?

He was completely confused. "Why would I need my wallet for a walk on the beach?" Suddenly, the light bulb went on. "You want to see if I'm carrying any protection! Well, I'm not. Because as I've told you, I don't sleep around. That's a big step, and one I don't take lightly."

She threw up her hands. "Then why did you spend all this time with me this week, and kiss me tonight like—like no other man ever has?"

He picked up the key card and jammed it in his pocket. "Maybe it was because I fell in love with you, Kelsea. Did you ever consider that?"

Landon walked out the door and slammed it behind him, closing the door to his heart.

31

BRANDON *LOVED* ME? I couldn't believe it. That was the last thing in the world I expected him to say. The words ricocheted around in my mind all night. I hardly slept, and welcomed my last sunrise on St. Jardin with a hundred-pound weight on my shoulders. I called housekeeping and asked for a broom and dustpan, cleaned up the flower mess, then tossed my last few items into my suitcase.

My stomach was in knots and I had no interest in breakfast, but I had to find Rose and Ike and say goodbye to them. It was a conversation I wasn't looking forward to.

I didn't see them anywhere in the main dining hall, and went back to the front desk. "Yes, they're in their office," the clerk said when I asked about them. He indicated an unmarked pink door across the lobby that stood slightly ajar.

"Hello?" I peeked in, and Rose's face brightened. I went in, and she greeted me with a hug. Today, she wore a flowing pink flowered muumuu and her ever-present Converse. Ike sat at his desk.

"Oh dear, Kelsea, I take it things didn't go well last night."

That's right, Brandon said Rose had given him the key card to my room. "How—did Brandon talk to you?"

"He was very concerned about you, dear."

"Well, it doesn't matter. Whatever did or didn't happen between us this week is over, and I'm going back to St. Louis, and he's going back to wherever he's from."

Rose and Ike exchanged a glance. "He didn't tell you anything about himself?"

I frowned. "No. What is it that you're not telling me?"

Rose rubbed my arm. "Kelsea, you've had a terrible couple of weeks, and your life has been turned upside down—what? About three times?"

Ike got up and came to stand beside his wife. "These things have a way of working out," he said. "Mine and Rose's path to the altar wasn't a straight one."

I smiled dimly. "Yes, she told me about it, Ike." I looked at these two people who had become so very dear to me, and reached for their hands. "Thank you so much for this week. I'll never forget it, and I'll never forget you." Tears rolled down my cheeks as I realized how much I would miss them. I knew I would never set foot on St. Jardin again, and the thought made me immensely sad.

Rose grasped both of my hands. "You are going to be fine, dear," she said. "Ike and I will be praying for you, and we *know* that we are going to see you again." That made me cry even harder.

They reached their arms around to hug me, and Rose whispered in my ear. "Remember, Kelsea Anderson, you're one of the strong ones."

32

LANDON STARED OUT the window of the plane. The first-class seat next to him sat empty, just as it had on the trip down. Then, it mirrored the empty space Nicola had left in his heart, but now, it hurt much worse because of the gaping hole left by Kelsea.

How could a woman whom he'd known only eight days turn his life so upside down?

When he discovered they were booked on the same flight, Landon had planned to arrange for Kelsea to sit next to him on the trip home. Instead, he'd pulled on a baseball cap, sunk into his jacket, and turned his face toward the window while the other passengers boarded. The fact that they were on the same flight to St. Louis was supremely ironic. *So near and yet so far.*

When they landed, he was the first one off the jet. He was hungry, so he went for a leisurely early dinner. He didn't want to chance running into Kelsea at baggage claim. When he was convinced enough time had passed, he went down and collected his bag.

He took an Uber home and walked through the frigid air to his front door. When he put the key in the deadbolt, he realized it wasn't engaged. He tried the knob and was relieved that it was locked. That could mean only one thing.

Landon walked into the entry and his gaze went immediately to the hall table. In the dim light he could make out a key, an envelope, and the ring that would be on his left hand now if things had gone differently. He looked at his bare ring finger. Both his and Kelsea's tri-gold wedding bands rested in his shirt pocket, next to his heart.

He set his bag down, picked up the envelope, and took out the notecard. Nicola's small, feminine script flowed across the page.

Dear Landon, I know you can never forgive me for leaving you at the altar. It was a cowardly way to handle things, and you deserved better. I think you know that things between us weren't what they should have been for a couple about to commit their lives to one another. That was my fault, too. I loved you, but I'm not sure I was ever in *love with you, if that makes any sense. I always suspected that I was part of the business deal between my father and your firm, and that's not a good foundation for a lasting relationship.*

I hold nothing against you, and wish you every happiness. Someday, I know that you will find a woman who loves you with her whole heart, and who is deserving of yours. Please, take this ring and my bridal set, and put them to good use. Have the engraving removed and then give them to someone, or sell them and use that to buy another ring when you meet that special woman.

It was signed simply, *Nicola.*

Landon took the note and the envelope, walked over to the gas fireplace, turned it on, and threw them in. Nicola had called her actions cowardly, but he realized that he'd been the coward by not being willing to confront her when he had serious doubts about their approaching marriage. He watched the paper burn until it was no more, and felt a weight lift from his shoulders. This chapter was completely closed. There was no need to meet with Nicola. There wasn't anything to say.

He walked into the kitchen and opened the fridge. He knew there was virtually nothing there, but came up with a can of soda. He popped it open and sat down at the counter on one of his bar stools, then made a call.

"Hello? Is that you, Landon?"

"Yeah, Dad, it's me. Just wanted you and Mom to know that I'm home."

"It's good to hear from you, son. Are you okay? We've been praying for you."

Landon smiled. "Thanks, Dad. I appreciate that."

"I hope it was a time of healing for you."

"In some ways it was, but something very unexpected also happened this week, Dad, and that's what I need to talk with you about."

Landon spent the next several minutes pouring out his heart about Kelsea. He told his dad how he felt when he was with her, how colors were more vivid, the air was fresher, and that he felt more alive than he ever had with Nicola. Landon said he couldn't explain it away by being in the tropical setting, he knew that it went beyond that. He told his dad about their common interests, about the things that he and Kelsea argued about, about her sharp wit and her strong opinions, and how just being around her made him feel like a better man.

He left out any reference to the ceremony at the Queen's Garden, or their kiss.

"It sounds like you're in love, son, for real this time," his father finally said.

"But it seems impossible," Landon protested. "What if it's not real, like a shipboard romance?"

"Trust your heart, son, despite the circumstances, despite how bad the timing is, despite how impossible it seems."

"But now, it looks like her former fiancé wants her back," Landon said, and shared everything that he knew about Ryan Singer, and about his and Kelsea's fight. He found himself choking up. "Dad, I can't lose her."

"I know you want to protect her, son, but she's got a lot to work through right now, and she needs to do it on her own. If you love her, you have to step back and give her the time and space to do that, so that when she comes to you, it will be with her whole heart."

Landon felt some of the burden lift. "Thanks, Dad. Someone else gave me similar advice. It won't be easy, but I know it's the right thing to do."

"I'll be praying for you, son, and you pray, too."

"Thanks, I will, Dad. I love you." Landon disconnected and sat where he was for quite a long time, not moving.

Finally, he admitted to himself that he couldn't be in control of this, and that he needed to leave it up to God.

33

WHEN WE LANDED in St. Louis, it was ten degrees and overcast. When the plane broke through the clouds on our descent, the sight of the stark, gray and white landscape settled around my heart like a heavy blanket. *Back to reality.*

I sat staring out the window while the other passengers filed out. I wasn't in a hurry to go anywhere. I was one of the last ones off the plane. By the time I hit the restroom in the terminal and shuffled down to baggage claim, most of the crowd had cleared. I grabbed my bag and headed for the door.

The subzero wind hit me like an icy freight train, and I sucked in a breath. *Would I ever feel warm again?* Fortunately, the shuttle to long-term parking was idling at the curb. I climbed aboard and found a seat.

"Oh, Myrtle," I said to my green VW bug when I reached it. "Let's get this ice scraped off." I started the engine to warm up. Myrtle was one of the new beetles, not a classic one. Her full name was Myrtle the Turtle.

My first stop was the kennel. I couldn't wait to see

Penny and Sheldon. I hadn't ever been away from them longer than overnight, and was afraid they had forgotten me. But I needn't have worried. Their enthusiastic welcome assured me that my dogs still loved me. It was a wonderful reunion.

We went straight home, and the first thing I did was turn up the heat and make a cup of tea. Then I changed into my softest, comfiest sleep clothes and my thickest socks.

I'm home, I texted to my mom and Morgan. That was our rule, anytime any of us traveled, that we'd notify the others when we were safely home. Almost instantly, my phone vibrated with a text. I really hoped it wasn't Mom. I wasn't up for a big conversation.

I breathed a sigh of relief when I saw Morgan's name. *Can we face time? Call me.* I sat down on my daybed, pulled the comforter up, and speed dialed her. "Hey Morgy, what's up?" I adjusted the screen and took a sip of my raspberry tea. *Perfect.*

"Hi. I just want to know how you're doing, Sissy." Morgan was the only person on the planet who was allowed to call me that. And I was sure that Dr. Morgan Anderson would *never* let anyone else call her Morgy. "I felt bad that I didn't come after the wedding was canceled. I was between semesters, so I could have."

"It's okay, really. I was such a mess, I wouldn't have been good company."

"How was St. Jardin?"

Sheldon and Penny hopped up to snuggle. "It was—not what I expected." *Understatement of the year.* "It's unbelievably beautiful, though." An image of the Queen's Garden in all its glory filled my senses. But that inevitably led to an image of Brandon and the fake marriage ceremony, and I needed to banish that.

"So, are you and Ryan getting back together?" Hesitancy filled my sister's voice.

"No," I said. "But I'm not mad that you told him where I was," I quickly added.

Relief showed visibly on her face. "Oh, that's good. But there must be more to the story. If you're not ready, I understand." I knew she was sincere. One of the best things about our sister relationship was that we had established firm boundaries years ago, and we both honored them.

I launched into the whole story, starting with general comments about the resort, Rose, Ike, and even a nameless jilted groom, then moving on to the details about Ryan's flowers and the drama that ensued—although nothing about Brandon's involvement and our fight. Morgan gasped when I told her about Jenna being pregnant.

"Kelsea! That's horrible! I never would have thought Ryan could do something like that!" Her long golden-brown hair, pulled high into a ponytail, bounced as she shook her head back and forth.

"I know. He had everyone fooled."

"Have you talked with him? Are you going to?"

"No, not yet. But I will. I want him to look me right in the eye and explain it, no matter how much it hurts. I'll text him tomorrow and set up a time to meet."

"So, tell me about this guy, the jilted groom that you got thrown together with on the island," Morgan said. Her eyes danced with anticipation. "Is he cute?"

Cute wasn't the thought that came to mind. *Try gorgeous, ripped, sexy, and overwhelmingly masculine, for starters.* "No, not really. And we were like oil and water. Not a good mix."

"Rose and Ike sound like a trip," she said with a laugh.

"Oh Morgy, they're just the cutest, sweetest people. Best friends and so in love after fifty-three years of marriage."

"Eww. I can't imagine being with one person for that long," Morgan groused. My sister was very career focused. I couldn't remember the last time that she dated anyone.

"When you meet the right guy, you'll change your tune," I said.

"Well, I don't see that happening." Morgan said. Something in her voice alerted my sister radar. There was something she wasn't saying. I just knew it.

"Because?" I prompted.

Silence settled in around me. Her eyes welled up. Then I heard her breath catch, like a little sob, and she began to cry.

"Morgan, what's wrong?"

"I, um, I've been having some issues," she said. My heartbeat accelerated. "Female issues. I haven't said anything to Mom about it, because, well, you know, she's Mom."

"I understand. I'm so sorry." I was really at a loss and didn't know what to say. "How serious is it?"

"It's not cancer or anything," Morgan reassured me, and I felt a wave of relief wash over me. She wiped her tears with a tissue, and her green eyes glistened like spring grass in the morning dew. "But the doctor says I probably won't ever be able to have children." I could hear the heartbreak in her voice.

My heart fell. "Oh, Morgan, I don't know what to say. I'm so sorry. Are they sure?"

"Pretty sure," she sighed. "I have to decide if I want them to do a procedure where they look around to know for sure. Right now I just need to get my pain under control. That was the main reason I didn't come to St. Louis when you canceled the wedding. I'm so sorry."

My eyes spilled over with tears. "You don't have anything to apologize for. I'm just so sorry that you're going through this. Is the pain bad?"

"It's getting a little better. I had to cut way back on some of my extra-curricular activities in the fall. They're adjusting my meds and hopefully I'll see a bigger improvement by the end of the month."

"Listen, Morgan." I cleared my throat. "You already have a very fulfilling career. If it *does* turn out that you can't have children, you can still meet a wonderful man and be very happy together. My friends Rose and Ike never had children." There was adoption, too, but I didn't feel that now was the time to get into that.

Her voice sounded small and scared. "I know, but it's hard to find a guy like that, you know? And I don't even know how that would work. I can't see myself on a first date saying, 'Hey, I'm damaged, I can't ever give you a child,' but if it starts getting serious, then how would I tell him? If I fall for a guy and then he walks away—"

"Hey, you're getting way ahead of yourself," I said. "Don't borrow trouble, like Mom always says."

"I know," she sighed, and swiped at her eyes again. "I just—I feel so old."

"I'm older than you!" I exclaimed, and we both laughed. "And now I'm back on the shelf, as they used to say."

"You'll be fine," Morgan said emphatically. "You'll end up marrying a great guy and have a whole houseful of kids."

"Well, I don't know where I'm going to meet any great

guys. Not in my line of work, anyway. And the clock is ticking," I muttered.

"Maybe you'll meet a cute vet," she said. I was happy to hear the lilt in her voice again. "And the one silver lining in my situation is that I'll have a valid excuse when Mom starts bugging me for grandkids."

"Ugh," I said. "I've got a lot of years before I'm off the hook for good."

"Well, sis," Morgan said, "go and let Ryan have it with both barrels, and then move on. If I can't be a mom, I want to be an aunt!"

"I love you, Morgy," I said.

"I love you, too, Sissy." She grinned. "Hey, we should do something during spring break. I know! We could go to St. Jardin! But not to that resort. There must be others."

"No thanks! I mean to St. Jardin. I'll always associate that place with honeymoons." *And a certain blond hunk who kissed like a dream.* "But we can go somewhere else. That would be fun."

"Awesome! I'll check out some ideas and e-mail you."

I told Morgan I loved her one more time, and disconnected. Penny and Sheldon had fallen asleep curled up in my lap. I buried my face in their soft fur, and thought about my sister. As successful a career as she had, I knew that she wanted to be a mother, to have a family. Both of us had held that deep desire for many years. It looked like that dream had slipped away for me, but it didn't have to for her.

"Dear God, please make a way for Morgan," I prayed.

I really meant to get up and unpack and do some

laundry, but Sheldon, Penny and I ended up falling asleep. An incoming call shook me awake, and I hit decline when I saw that it was Ryan. It was after six o'clock. I had no desire to talk with him. In a few seconds, he sent a text.

Are you home? I've been thinking about you all day.

I took a deep breath. I wasn't ready to drop my bombshell on him, so I would need to appear cordial.

Yes, I'm back.

I can't wait to see you. Dinner tonight at eight? Le Bistro?

I snorted. The romantic French restaurant that we called *our place?* Not on your life. *I can't. Coffee, tomorrow morning at 11, Tillie's. I'll fit you in between appointments.* That was a bald-faced lie, but he didn't need to know that. I needed to make the point, now, that he was no longer first in my life. Tomorrow he would know in no uncertain terms that he no longer had *any* place in my life.

Can I please come over tonight?

No, I'm going to bed now. Super tired. See you tomorrow. I turned my phone off, and went to the kitchen to figure something out for dinner. Ritz crackers and peanut butter counted as a two-course meal, right?

I went straight back to bed, slept fitfully, and woke up with a headache. A cup of peppermint tea and massaging peppermint oil on my temples took care of it, but I was jumpy and didn't feel like eating anything. Not that there was anything to eat in my apartment. The grocery store would be my first stop after meeting with Ryan.

Since I hadn't gotten to it last night, I decided to unpack and start a load of laundry. As soon as I unzipped my suitcase, the aroma of tropical flowers wove itself around me. My eyes filled with tears. Right on top where I had wrapped them in a plastic bag lay my crown and Brandon's lei, and the little nosegay of red and white roses that he had chosen for me. They were crushed and wilted, but still amazingly fragrant. I buried my nose in them and closed my eyes. Memories of being with Brandon at the Queen's Garden assaulted me, and I was filled with a deep sense of sadness.

I spent the morning trying to keep busy but not accomplishing anything, willing the clock to move along, and finally left my apartment at 10:45. I hadn't taken any pains with my appearance. I didn't want Ryan to think that I was trying to impress him. I wore jeans, boots, and an oversized teal cable-knit sweater. My hair was up in a messy bun, and my makeup consisted of a little mascara and my favorite vanilla mint lip balm.

I cruised into Tillie's and chose a table near the door. I wanted to be able to make a quick exit. A swirl of heavenly scents surrounded me, and my stomach rumbled in protest. I ordered comfort food—a cup of hot chocolate and a blueberry muffin.

As soon as I got settled, Ryan came through the door. He leaned down and tried to kiss me, but I turned my head just in time for his lips to make awkward contact with my cheek.

He shrugged out of his coat and sat down. "Wow, Kels, you look good. You got some sun."

Ryan's dark, good looks suddenly didn't seem so attractive to me. The descriptor *smarmy, oily cheat* leapt to mind.

"Yes, a week in the Caribbean usually does that." I took a bite of muffin and it all but melted in my mouth.

"Well, um, I—wow, Kels, I've missed you."

I kept chewing and stared at him, but stayed silent. I wanted to see what kind of trouble he'd talk himself into. If there was one thing I knew about Ryan, it was that he couldn't keep quiet for long.

He didn't disappoint. "So, I guess you've been wondering about me, about us, about—" he laughed nervously. "About how we're going to pick up and go on. Because I really do want us to, you know, go on." He seemed to be waiting for me to say something.

This is kind of fun. I took a leisurely sip of my cocoa and kept quiet.

"I guess you're waiting for me to say I'm sorry. I really am sorry, Kels. I know my timing was terrible, but I just got cold feet, you know? So, ah, if you still want to get married, let's go ahead and plan that. I'm ready now. I'm really ready. We can have the fall wedding you always wanted."

When pigs fly. I wanted to spin this out. I wiped my mouth with my napkin, picked up a spoon, and stirred my cocoa. Then I took another bite of my delicious muffin, chewed, and swallowed.

"Who's Jenna Harmon?" I said matter-of-factly.

I really wish I'd taken a video of his reaction. Ryan's face blanched white, and he put his head in his hands and groaned. Then, he quickly recovered. "Kelsea, I can explain. It's not what it looks like."

I took another sip of cocoa. "That's interesting, Ryan, because it *looks like* the minute I left town for Thanksgiving, you hooked up with Jenna. And now she's pregnant."

He ran his fingers over his face and up through his dark brown hair, then let out a loud breath.

"I—Kelsea, I, yes, it was a huge mistake, and I really

141

didn't know what I was doing. A bunch of us went out on Wednesday night after work, and I, you know, drank a little too much, and somehow ended up going back to Jenna's apartment with her. I never stopped loving you, it was just—a big mistake."

Ryan reached for my hand, but I pulled it away before he could make contact. "You never stopped loving me." I drenched every syllable with sarcasm. "Gee, Ryan, how does that work, when you're in bed with another woman? You're thinking, 'I love my fiancée so much, even though I've never slept with *her*.'" I crossed my arms over my chest and stared at him. "Please, tell me how that works, Ryan." My voice was cold and clipped.

"Kels, I'm—I'm so sorry. I know we said we would wait. I just—"

"You said that it would make our marriage more sacred, more meaningful."

"It still can be," he implored, his voice low and impassioned.

I wanted to scream, but after all, we were in public. "Are you kidding me, Ryan? You think I'm going to plan a wedding to you while you're *in a relationship* with Jenna? While she's carrying your child?" I was done here. I started to push my chair back.

He sat up straighter and reached out his hand again, and found nothing but air. "But that's just it, Kelsea. I—it happened *just that one time.* Then she put on my page that we were in a relationship. I took it down as soon as I saw it. It wasn't even up there for thirty minutes."

Wow. How serendipitous was it that Brandon happened to click on Ryan's page during that short window of time.

I crossed my arms in front of me. "But it's up on *her* page."

"That was all a big—plan on her part to make her boyfriend jealous. She never cared anything about me," Ryan spat. "We're *not* in a relationship. I don't know why she won't take it down. She put his name back up, and now it's back to mine, but I don't know why. She won't answer any of my calls or texts."

Oh, poor, poor Ryan! Cue the violins.

"Is the baby yours?"

He shook his head, looking more miserable. "I don't know. Right after we—right after Thanksgiving, he came running back to her, and then she turned up pregnant just after Christmas." He swallowed. "She doesn't know who the father is, but she says she has some of my DNA from when I was at her apartment, and she's going to have a paternity test done when the baby's born."

I didn't want to even contemplate what comprised the DNA sample.

"So if the child isn't yours, you're off the hook. And if it is, she'll stick you for half of all her medical bills, and child support for the next eighteen years."

He nodded, looking utterly miserable. He hung his head. "I know I don't deserve another chance, Kelsea."

"You're absolutely right, and you're not getting one, Ryan. You had *one job*. To be faithful to me. And you failed. I could never, *ever* trust you again."

"Kels—" his tortured eyes begged.

I was completely disgusted with him. I collected my jacket and stood. "Goodbye, Ryan. I kind of hope the baby is yours. Maybe parenthood will force you to grow up."

"Kelsea, wait. I—"

If he was going to beg again, I might lose my cocoa and blueberry muffin.

Ryan clambered to his feet. "Well, if you're not going to—could I—" He scratched his head. "Well, I was wondering, could I have my ring back?"

I stood there frozen, unable to move. "*Your* ring? It's *my* ring," I said in the iciest voice I could dredge up. No way was I telling him that I sold it.

"Well, I think there's a legal—law or something about that. And it would help, um, pay my mom back for some of the deposits—"

I wasn't listening to another word. "Don't ever try to contact me again, Ryan, or I *will* take legal action." I'd never hired an attorney and had no idea how I would afford one, but he didn't need to know that. I enunciated each word, turned my back to him, and walked away, holding my head high.

I spent the rest of the day running errands in an attempt to stay busy. Every time I thought about Ryan and his outrageous demand that I return the ring, I got steamed up all over again.

The next day, I went back to work. It was good to be back in my routine, and I almost had more work than I could handle. I was too busy to think about Ryan and what my life would have been now as a married woman.

We always have a January thaw in St. Louis, and a couple of days later, the temperature soared up to the high fifties. I knew it was a temporary reprieve, so I moved my schedule around so I could go to the dog park. I took Sheldon, Penny, and two client dogs with me, and was happy to see my friend Maggie there with Duke the Scottish terrier and Lucky the golden retriever.

We exchanged a hug. "How are you doing, Kelsea?" she asked, tucking her auburn hair under her cap as the temperate breeze played havoc with it. She was probably ten or twelve years older than me.

I shrugged. "I'm okay." I said. "Believe it or not, I went on our honeymoon, alone." I explained how I'd come to that decision, and a little bit about St. Jardin.

"Good for you, girl!" Maggie said, squeezing my arm. "I've heard that island is beautiful, but I never knew anyone who went there."

"It's unbelievably gorgeous," I said. "And it was so good to get away from winter. My mom thought I should use the time to figure out a Plan B, but I never really got around to it."

Maggie nodded. "Are you going to keep doing your pet business?"

"Definitely," I said. "I'm thankful I have a great place to live, and I get to work with animals. I almost have more business than I can handle, thanks to you."

She waved her hand. "Oh, I didn't do anything. Just sang your praises to a few friends. You're the one who earned your good reputation."

We chatted for another little while and watched the dogs frolic. "Let's walk," Maggie suggested. There was a beautiful paved trail next to a pond. We made one loop around, and as we were getting ready to go our separate ways, a stocky man with medium-brown hair approached us. "Is one of you Kelsea Anderson?" he asked pleasantly.

"That would be me," I said.

"The one with the pet business?"

Maggie and I exchanged a smile. A client was seeking me out! "Yes. Do you have a dog that needs walked or something?"

"Yeah, I might," he said, taking a piece of paper out of his pocket. "Could you just write your name and phone number on this?"

I scribbled the information down and handed it back to him. "Great," he said. Then he drew out an envelope and handed it to me. "Thanks, Kelsea Anderson, you've been served."

My jaw dropped, and Maggie and I stared at each other as the man turned and left without another word. "What was that all about?" she exclaimed.

"I have a bad feeling about this," I muttered, tearing the envelope open. It was worse than I feared. "Ryan is suing me for the engagement ring, or its fully appraised value in cash, and—" I gasped. "I don't believe it." I thrust the papers at Maggie.

She gasped. "He's suing you for *half* the cost of everything associated with the wedding? He's the one who pulled out!"

"*And* the reception!" I stomped my foot furiously. I couldn't believe this. "That lying scumbag—you don't even know the whole story!" I felt tears pricking at my eyes.

"I've got time to listen if you want to talk."

I looked at my phone. "I'd love to, but I've got to get these guys back to their house." Tears threatened to spill.

Maggie patted my arm. "Why don't you come to my house after? I'd really like to help you figure this out, Kelsea."

I was so thankful for Maggie's friendship, and nodded. "That would be—nice, thank you. What was your address again?" It had been over a year since I'd looked after Duke and Lucky.

"We're on La Bonne Terrace, 169."

"I'll take these dogs home, and then drop Sheldon and Penny at my apartment."

"Great, see you soon." She gave me a hug.

"Thanks so much, Maggie."

The first time I came to Maggie's house, I was surprised to discover that she lived right across the street from *The Victorian.* That's what I called it, anyway, a gorgeous home that sat on an acre of land. There were other beautiful homes in this eclectic neighborhood, but The Victorian outshone them all. It became my dream home from the moment I saw it when I'd first moved to Kirkwood and started taking Sheldon and Penny on walks.

I rang Maggie's doorbell and she answered almost immediately. "Come in, come in," she said. "I'm so glad you came. I just made tea. Would you like some?" She took my coat and hung it on the coat tree. I followed her into a cozy breakfast nook just off the kitchen, where I could smell bread baking.

"You live across the street from *The Victorian,*" I commented as we sat and fixed our tea. "That's what I call it. That's my dream house."

Maggie smiled. "Have you ever been inside?"

I nodded. "Yes, about two years ago when it was for sale. I went to one of the open house events. I couldn't resist."

"That's when I went inside it, too, when we were looking at houses." Maggie and I spent several minutes talking about all the things we both loved about the house.

"Did you consider buying it?" I asked.

Maggie shook her head. "Melissa was already off to college by then, and Mike and I knew that it was too much house and yard for just the two of us. This one was perfect for us."

I looked around the warm room. "It's beautiful," I said. "I still have every square foot of the Victorian memorized." Maggie laughed. "I always told Ryan that he could buy that house for me for our tenth anniversary. I figured we would have a couple of children by then and would need the space." To my surprise, a deep sense of melancholy washed over me.

Maggie took a sip of her tea. "So, tell me the rest of the story about Ryan, if it will help."

I dove in, and didn't leave out any details. She was aghast, and repeatedly assured me that as painful as it was, that I was better off without him, and I knew she was right. My heart was completely over the louse.

"But now, this lawsuit," I said. I put my head in my hands. "I have no idea what I'm going to do about it. The court date is in a little over a week, on my birthday." *Brandon's birthday.* I tried to push that thought out of my mind.

"Oh, no! That's adding insult to injury!" Maggie exclaimed.

"I suppose I should hire a lawyer," I said, "but I have no idea how to go about that. And the timing is terrible. I haven't had time to replenish my savings after paying for the honeymoon. I don't know what I'm going to do."

"Listen," Maggie said. "My husband is an attorney. He specializes in corporate law, so he doesn't work directly with things like this, but maybe he'll have some ideas." She looked at the clock. "Oh, it's almost six."

I pushed my chair back. "I'm sorry, I didn't realize it was so late. I'll be going now."

Maggie put her hand on my arm. "Kelsea, no, that's not what I meant. Mike will be home soon. Please stay and have dinner with us, and we can tell him all about this and maybe he can think of a solution."

"Are you sure?" I asked.

Maggie stood and went to the stove. "Absolutely. We're just having soup and bread tonight."

I followed her, and leaned against the island. "The bread smells delicious."

We kept chatting, and before long, a man came through the door from the garage. He was in his late forties, balding, with glasses and an engaging smile. Maggie greeted him and made the introductions. "This is Kelsea Anderson. My husband, Mike Porter. Kelsea's staying for dinner."

"That's great," he said. I liked Mike right away. "I'm happy to meet you, Kelsea," he said with a warm smile.

We all chatted while I helped Maggie get dinner on the table in the little nook, and we held hands. Mike prayed, thanking God for His provision, for the food, and for the privilege of having their friend Kelsea in their home. I realized that I couldn't remember the last time anyone had thanked God for me, and a peaceful feeling settled over me.

We made small talk for a while, chatted about dogs and the neighborhood and my business. The soup and bread were amazing—I told Maggie she should open a restaurant! And then she told Mike about my dilemma—leaving out the dramatic parts—and encouraged me to talk, which I did.

When I finally got to the part about the lawsuit, Mike asked some thoughtful questions. "The ring could go either way," he said, "depending on who he hires to represent him. I think you've got the advantage on the costs for the wedding and reception, if you didn't have a hand in actually making those arrangements."

"I didn't," I insisted. "His mother chose everything and managed all the details. She even set the date."

Maggie had gotten up and was dishing up ice cream at the island. She rolled her eyes. "She sounds like a nightmare."

Mike rocked his hand back and forth in so-so motion. "The problem is, you'll get mired down in a "he said/she said" scenario. He could say that his mother made the arrangements, but *you* were the one who chose everything, and insisted on everything, so you should be responsible for half the cost."

"Even though *he* was the one who called off the wedding?"

"That doesn't seem fair," Maggie murmured. She set down bowls of ice cream for everyone.

Mike patted her hand. "Honey, you know the law isn't always about what's fair." He looked at me. "It depends on whether or not there's some dirt there, and if you want to find it. About the reason he backed out."

Maggie and I exchanged a look. I didn't know if I wanted to go down that road, or even if there was enough of a road to go down. "How does that work?" I asked Mike.

"Well, you hire a defense attorney, who hires a private

investigator to dig into what Ryan's been up to for the last six months or so—or you could hire a PI on your own."

I felt hopeless. "The real problem is, I don't really have any money saved to hire either one." I asked Mike a ballpark idea of what a defense attorney might cost, and almost fell out of my chair at the figure he quoted. I had been thinking of *maybe* asking my mom for a loan, but it was completely out of the question.

"The other option you have is the Public Defender's Office." He explained how that would work, and I saw a dim glimmer of hope. I didn't really have another option. "When's your trial date?"

"January 28."

He grimaced. "That's coming up quickly. They didn't give you much time. Probably part of their strategy. You don't know who he hired to represent him?"

"No idea. If his mother's behind it, probably a big, tough law firm."

Mike pulled a pen and a business card from his shirt pocket. "I know a guy over at the PD's office." He scribbled on the back of it and handed it to me. "Here's my card. Ask for him and tell him I referred you. I can't guarantee anything, but maybe it will help. And if you run into a wall, call me and I'll see if there's anything else I can do."

I thanked him sincerely, and asked Maggie if I could help her clean up.

She gave me a hug. "Absolutely not. This will take five minutes to get in the dishwasher." They walked me to the front door.

"Thank you so much," I said. They told me to keep them updated, and to stop by any time. I felt warmed by their friendship and the simple home cooked meal that they'd shared with me. I should really learn to cook real food, but when you live alone, it's hardly worth the trouble, and then you have all those leftovers.

Maggie stepped out onto the porch with me, and looked around in the darkness. "Where's your car? Did you walk?"

"I did," I said. "The weather was so nice today."

"Oh, let Mike run you home, Kelsea."

"No, absolutely not. Really, Maggie, I want to walk. I have some thinking to do."

"Do you have your mace?"

I grinned and held up my key ring. "Right here."

"Okay then, that makes me feel better. I'm so glad you came." She waved goodbye and I headed down the walk.

The Victorian was right in front of me, beautifully lit up. It looked utterly peaceful and so perfect. I stopped at the end of the sidewalk and stared at it. This was a home for a family, and I imagined a loving mom and dad inside with their children. They had probably just finished dinner. They would be helping the kids with their homework in the great room with the fireplace, or maybe playing a game together before baths and story time and then bedtime.

A tear trickled down one cheek. Earlier today, living in a studio apartment with Sheldon and Penny and walking dogs had seemed like enough. Suddenly, my life felt very empty.

34

LANDON FINALLY GOT the last of the boxes out to the curb. He was relieved to be done with moving. Hopefully, this would be it for a while.

When he'd arrived back from St. Jardin, his condo no longer held any appeal for him. It was right downtown, too noisy, and reminded him of Nicola. He swore her scent still lingered.

He contacted a realtor and put it on the market, fully furnished. A sale was already pending. He ended up finding a great starter home in a suburb just west of Kirkwood. Landon wanted to be closer to Kelsea and intended to make her a much bigger part of his life. He'd thought about looking right in Kirkwood, but didn't want to chance running into her yet, especially if she decided not to make a future with him. The house was a good investment and he could fix it up and flip it if necessary. *Stop thinking that way.*

Landon paused for a few moments to look at the front of his house. It was a foreclosure, which was why he was able to close on it so quickly and move in. Once spring arrived, he couldn't wait to get busy in the yard. There was a lot of work to do, and he hoped Kelsea would be by his side.

He still didn't know how or when he was going to contact her, but an idea had occurred to him just last night. Landon wanted to think and pray about it before making a decision.

Just as he walked into the kitchen, his cell vibrated on the counter. It was his brother. "Hey, man," he answered.

"Hey, man," Brandon echoed. Landon felt a twinge of discomfort. He hadn't shared yet that he'd "borrowed" his brother's name when he was on St. Jardin, and wasn't sure if he ever would. "What's shakin'?"

"Not much. I was just thinking about you, and thought I'd give a call. How's the new house?"

"It's good. Feels good to be out of that condo. Too many memories."

"Yeah, she decorated it and all, didn't she?"

"Um-hmm." Landon started sorting piles of clothes to put in the dresser drawers.

"When you have a big break-up like that, sometimes it's good to just start over again with a clean slate."

Landon chuckled. "Like you'd know?" Brandon had married his high school sweetheart, Darla.

"Well, that's what I've heard," Brandon replied with a laugh.

"How's my niece?"

"She's great." Landon could hear the deep pride in his brother's voice. "I love being a dad. Can't wait for our second daughter to get here." Darla was about seven months along now.

"You guys are gonna have your hands full," Landon said.

"I know, but it's okay. We got started late." Brandon and Darla were both doctors and had waited to start a family until they'd gotten through med school and residency.

Landon smiled. "I'm happy for you, bro."

"Mom would be happy if you gave her some grandchildren, too," Brandon said.

"Yeah, I'm sure, but she's going to have to wait now." Their older sister, Reagan, was completely career-focused and had no interest in a husband or children, and their younger sister, Sara, was in college and trying to figure out what she wanted out of life.

"And one of us needs to make sure the St. Clair name will go on."

Landon snorted. "That's your department, bro."

Brandon laughed. "We'll see. So, anyone on your radar?"

"What do you think?" Landon retorted. He was certain that his father wouldn't have broken his confidence. His brother wouldn't believe it if he said that he'd already fallen in love and picked out his next bride, and after the debacle with Nicola, Landon didn't think he'd let a word slip to a soul until the marriage was legal. But how would that work, to give Kelsea the wedding she deserved with no one in attendance? *Slow down, man. Take it one step at a time. She's not even speaking to you.*

"Hey! Bro, you still there?"

"Sorry," Landon squeezed the bridge of his nose. "I was just looking at something in the backyard."

"Well, I'll let you go. I just wanted to check up on you.

Come for a visit when you can." Brandon and Darla lived in Minnesota, where it was winter for at least six months of the year.

"Yeah, maybe in the summer," Landon replied.

"And don't hesitate to call if you need to talk, anytime," Brandon said.

Landon laughed. "When? You work a hundred hours a week."

"Not so much anymore," Brandon protested. "I'm down to eighty. Love ya, man."

"Love ya, man."

Landon had a great family and was very fortunate for their support at this time in his life. He couldn't wait for Kelsea to meet them. He stuffed his phone into his pocket and went to tackle the bedroom that was going to be his office. Soon, he had his desk organized and fired up his laptop. It had been a couple of days since he'd checked his personal e-mail.

Aww...look at that! Landon chuckled and opened the e-mail, and his entire world shifted on its axis.

35

MY PHONE WOKE me up at 6:30, and for a moment, I was disoriented. For the third time this week, I had dreamed of walking hand-in-hand with Brandon along the sea shore. And this time, he was just about to kiss me.

I looked at my phone. *Mom.* This was my birthday call. It was the last thing I felt like celebrating, but she had no idea about the lawsuit, and I had no intention of bringing it up. Depending on the outcome, I might never have to.

I've always thought that someone's birthday should be as much about their parents as about them. After all, it was one of the most joyful days of their life. With every passing year, I missed my dad more and more. And even though my mother annoyed me to no end at times, I loved her, and was truly thankful for her.

I took a breath. "Hi, Mom," I said cheerily.

"Happy Birthday, Kelsea Denise!" she cried. "I can't believe my baby girl is thirty!"

I winced. "Me neither," I said. "It sounds so old." *Especially when you're a spinster with no prospects.*

"Then what does that make me?" Mom lamented. We chatted for a while, and she wrapped up the call saying that she had sent me a check "to buy yourself a little something special." She didn't mention anything about my present circumstances, and I appreciated that.

After I hung up, I grabbed my coat and slippers to take the dogs out. Our January thaw was completely over. We'd gotten snow over the past two days, and the overnight temps were back in the single digits.

When I opened the back door, I almost tripped over something. A cardboard box? I couldn't imagine who had left that. It was long and narrow, but not too heavy. There were no markings on it.

I stuck it inside and hurried down the stairs with Sheldon and Penny to do their business. When we got back inside, I tossed off my coat and carried the box to the table and opened it. Inside was a Styrofoam container. I pulled it open and was shocked to see two dozen beautiful red and white roses.

I picked them up and inhaled their scent. *Oh, heavenly. These didn't come from the grocery store.* I searched for a card, and finally saw it. If they weren't from Mom, they were probably from Morgan. But how did it get delivered, and by whom? I looked carefully at the outer box again, but there were no markings on it.

I opened the card, and the blood rushed to my head. The neat, block printing swam before my eyes. *Happy Birthday, Kelsea. You know who this is. I've thought of no one and nothing but you since we left St. Jardin. I know it seems impossible, and it doesn't make sense, but I knew even before we went to the Queen's Garden that I had fallen in love with you. I know I made a lot of mistakes, the worst one being that I lied to you about my name, and never told you anything about myself. I had my reasons, and had every intention of doing that on our last night there, but we both know that didn't happen.*

My heart pounded, and I began to cry. *Lied to you about my name?* This was impossible. It seemed that I could only fall for men who were allergic to the truth. I read on. *Will you meet me tonight at 7pm at Union Station, at the entrance to the indoor lake? I promise to tell you everything then— everything about me. You can ask any questions you want, and I'll answer them. Please, wear the beautiful green dress that you wore the first night we met at the resort. I hope this is the first of many birthdays together. I love you. Please, come tonight.*

My eyes roamed over the page again, but kept going back to two phrases, *I had fallen in love with you,* and *I love you.*

I closed my eyes and thought about our kiss on St. Jardin. I'd relived it hundreds of times over the last three weeks. I missed Brandon—or whoever he was—so much.

I dried my tears and jumped up. I couldn't think about this right now. I had dogs to walk and two houses to check on, fish to feed (not to mention cleaning the aquarium), a cat to take to the groomer's, and then the blasted court case at two o'clock. So much was riding on it. Maggie was coming over at noon to do my makeup. If I couldn't be confident about the case or my defense, at least I would be dressed for success.

I fingered the card again. I couldn't seem to let go of it. How did he get the roses here? Of course he knew my name, so he could find out where I lived. But did he deliver them himself, or have someone do it for him? If he was hoping to meet me tonight, he must be in town, or on his way. This was crazy. I had no idea who he was, or where he lived, or what he did for a living.

Could I commit myself to a man that I knew so little about? And was I ready to trust someone again? I tucked the card into my purse. I couldn't think about this now.

36

"HAPPY BIRTHDAY, BOSS." Landon's executive assistant, Pam, greeted him when he arrived at the office. "There's bagels and pastries in the break room."

"Thanks, Pam," he replied with a smile. She was his right arm and always honored Landon's wish not to make a big deal about his birthday.

He'd felt like a cat burglar when he snuck up the back stairs to Kelsea's apartment at o'dark hundred and left the box for her. He was worried about alerting her dogs. If Sheldon or Penny had started barking, he had no idea what he would have done.

Thankfully, his schedule for today was jam packed. He had about twelve hours until he would know whether Kelsea was willing to move forward with him. But he had a lot to do before then, and settled into his large, leather chair to begin the workday. He had two meetings and a conference call, and managed to power through the morning, which helped pass the time. He ate a salad for lunch at his desk and started working on a brief that was due next week.

Landon looked at his watch and sighed. It was three minutes later than the last time he had checked. He rubbed a hand over his face. *Tonight, I'll see her. I've missed her so much. Please, God, let her come. Let her heart soften so that we have a chance at happiness. I love her more than I ever thought possible.*

He had to get this brief done, but his mind wasn't on it. It kept straying to ways that he could get through to Kelsea if she didn't show. Had she liked the roses? He could buy her a hundred dozen more. Maybe he would take them right to her apartment and refuse to leave until he could get through to her.

Landon got up from his desk and walked over to where he'd hung up his brand new suit jacket. He'd never spent so much on a suit, but tonight would be the most important night of his life, the first of many birthdays that he hoped with all his heart that he and Kelsea would celebrate together.

Landon slipped his hand into the inner pocket and drew out their tri-gold wedding bands, and a 1.75-karat solitaire diamond in a rose gold setting. The brilliant, flawless stone sparkled in the early afternoon sun. Landon intended for it to blind every man who came within a mile of his woman.

The phone on his desk rang, and he quickly returned the rings and reached for the receiver. "Landon St. Clair."

It was the top second-year associate on his team, Sean Busch. "Landon, it's Sean." He sounded out of breath. "Olivia's water just broke. Her mother is driving her to the hospital. I'm in the car, on my way to meet them."

Landon thought the couple's first baby wasn't due for a while yet, and Sean's next words confirmed his fears. "She's only at thirty three weeks," he said, his voice cracking. "I'm due in court at two o'clock, but I have to go."

"Of course you do, Sean, don't worry about it. Are you sure you're okay?"

"I sure could use some prayers right about now."

"You got it. And I'll take your case. Where's the file?"

"On my desk. I'm working on three cases right now. This one is Singer vs. Anderson. We're representing the plaintiff, Ryan Singer."

37

I WAITED OUTSIDE the courtroom for my attorney. I didn't have a clue what to expect. I just knew it would be someone from the Public Defender's office, whoever had been assigned to my case. I was thankful that Mike had referred me, but I wondered if I should have taken out a loan or figured out a way to hire a better lawyer. Oh well, it was too late now.

I wore a black pencil skirt, black-and-white polka dot pumps with a sweet white bow on top, and a red cashmere sweater over a white shell. I'd spent more than I should have last night to have my hair trimmed and styled. It fell past my shoulders in shiny, perfect layers, and Maggie's magic with a makeup brush had produced phenomenal results. I looked good and I knew it.

"Ms. Anderson?" a male voice cracked on the last syllable. I looked up to see a painfully skinny thirteen-year-old dressed for his first dance, right down to his slicked-back hair. Actually, I feared that this was my attorney. My heart dropped to my feet. This was probably his first case.

I stood, looming over him in my heels. I stuck out my hand, and he pumped it with his clammy one. "I'm Anson Greene," he said. "Your lawyer."

I wanted to ask him if his mother had dropped him off at the courthouse, but instead, dredged up a smile. "Pleased to meet you, Mr. Greene."

He laughed nervously. "Oh, no one has ever called me that. You can call me Anson." He just stood there.

I looked around, then glanced at the clock, which read 1:54. "Should we go in?" I asked.

Anson Greene looked startled. "Sure! I mean, yes, we should. Go in." He rushed over to the door, and we did an awkward shuffle as he stepped in front of me, opened it, and gestured for me to enter.

This was it. I was about to go to battle with Ryan. Rose's voice played in my head. *You're one of the strong ones.*

I threw my shoulders back and stood tall and proud. My mind went back to the days when Morgan and I would spend rainy afternoons practicing walking like queens with a book on our heads. I sailed down the main aisle of the courtroom as if it were Westminster Abbey, with my page—er, lawyer—trailing along behind me.

Suddenly, I realized that I didn't have a clue where to go. I called on my expertise, formed by many years of watching TV courtroom dramas, and decided that we would be on the left side of the courtroom, the judge's right.

I was so proud of myself for figuring this out that I didn't see Ryan approach. He inserted himself between Mr. Greene and me and tugged on my arm.

"Kelsea, can we talk?" he whispered.

I looked down at his hand, and back at his face.

"Remove your hand, now." I said in a cold voice. "I have nothing to say to you, now or ever."

"Kelsea, please. It was my mom. It was all my mom."

"Your mother got Jenna pregnant? I'd love to have seen that."

Ryan's face twisted and he closed his eyes. "No, of course not. I told you, that was—a huge mistake. And one way or another, I'll be paying for it the rest of my life."

"Yeah, some actions have long-term consequences, Ryan. Goodbye."

He held fast to my arm. "Kelsea, this lawsuit was all my mom's idea—"

"Mr. Singer! Unhand my client at once!" Anson Greene shouted. His face was…well, I never understood what the color *puce* was until now. Ryan jumped back, startled.

I ignored the murmurs rippling through the courtroom and resumed my regal walk to our table. *Who are these commoners, anyway, and why do they care about this case?* I sat down, crossed my ankles in what I hoped was the picture of demureness, set my purse on the table, and folded my hands in my lap. The epitome of calm. I turned to my lawyer, who was a hot mess, and dipped my chin. "Thank you, Mr. Greene," I murmured. Maybe there was some steel in him, after all.

On the inside, I seethed. Of all the—how could I have not seen how much of a mama's boy Ryan was? I suppose I had been blinded by love, to the point that I didn't even see through Jasmine Singer's controlling machinations. I thought she was just being generous and kind to manage all the details. I fell for it hook, line, and sinker.

I couldn't wait for this to be over. I rubbed some

peppermint oil on my pounding temples and spread another drop inside my mouth to freshen my breath. I still had to decide whether or not to meet what's-his-name tonight. Part of me wanted to, but part of me was still so confused and scared. I just needed to get through this afternoon, and then I could make a final decision.

"All rise," the bailiff intoned. "Call to order the Court of the City of St. Louis. The Honorable Lawrence D. Williamson presiding."

After we sat, Anson Greene splashed water into a plastic cup and took a gulp. His face had faded to tomato red. "Want some?"

"No, thank you." The judge was looking through some papers and seemed to be waiting for something. "Who's the plaintiff's attorney?" I whispered.

Anson opened his briefcase, which was full of papers. He started pulling them out haphazardly, and several fluttered to the floor. He gathered them up, rifled through them, and frowned.

"Jacoby, James, and something, I think," he said. Then he held up a sheet of paper. "Ah! Here it is." I took the paper from him.

Jacoby, Jamison & St. Clair. I nearly groaned out loud. Anson Greene must not be from the area. JJS was the very best law firm in St. Louis, a legal powerhouse with an astonishingly high success rate. That's all. Of course Jasmine Singer would have hired them. What was I doing, sitting here with Beaver Cleaver? This was a David vs. Goliath match-up if there ever was one.

The legalese swam before my eyes. None of it made a lick of sense. I glanced at my attorney, who was already sweating. I was doomed. JJS was a huge firm with lots of resources, even though I was sure this little case would go to one of their junior associates. I scanned the partners' names at the top of the letterhead. *Jeffrey M. Jacoby. Paul R. Jamison. Landon P. St. Clair.*

Something sounded familiar about one of those names. I read them again. Hmm…Landon St. Clair. Why did that ring a bell?

Brandon St. Fair.

No. It couldn't be.

The judge looked at the clock. "Mr. Singer, it's now 2:05. I don't know where your attorney is, but we can't wait any longer. We'll have to reschedule." I had refused to look at Ryan and was surprised to see him sitting alone at the plaintiff's table.

"But Your Honor—" Ryan sputtered.

I heard the door in the rear of the courtroom open, and strong, resolute footsteps echoed on the tile floor.

"Landon St. Clair, JJS, for the defense, Your Honor. I apologize for being late."

That voice. I would know it anywhere. That voice had lived in my head and filled my dreams since I had left St. Jardin. That voice had moved me to joyous laughter and to tears of frustration. That voice had shouted at me in exasperation and whispered sweetly in my ear. My heart went into wild palpitations.

Brandon St. Fair was really Landon St. Clair? He was the S in JJS? He lived and worked in St. Louis? My head was spinning. Anson Greene looked like the proverbial deer in the headlights.

Ryan was incredulous. "What do you mean, for the

defense? I don't know who you are, or where my attorney is, but JJS is representing me!" he shouted. Then my brain caught up with reality. The tall, outrageously handsome attorney had stated he was *for the defense.*

"Actually, we're not." He strode confidently through the bar and approached the bench, addressing the judge in a loud, clear voice. "Mr. Singer is no longer our client. I'm here to represent the defendant."

I waited for my lawyer to do something. But he just sat there, his mouth opening and closing like a fish.

I almost stood to object. *Can the defendant do that?* I didn't have a prayer of being able to afford an attorney from JJS, let alone a partner. He probably made more in an hour than I made in two weeks.

"You can't do that!" Jasmine Singer screamed as she shot to her feet just behind Ryan. Her Botox-infused face twisted into one big grimace.

"Sit down, Mrs. Singer," Judge Williamson ordered.

"Yes, I can." Landon St. Clair said calmly. He handed a thin, tidy sheaf of papers to the judge. "It's summarized in this brief, Your Honor. There's precedence for extenuating circumstances."

Judge Williamson perused the papers and frowned. "I understand the allowance due to extenuating circumstances, but this is highly unusual, Counselor. Why would you change your representation from the plaintiff to the defendant?"

For the first time since entering the room, the man I knew as Brandon made direct eye contact with me. No more baboon, no more gopher, no more dweeb. He was the most handsome man I had ever seen in my life. Tall and tan, broad and blond in an impeccably tailored charcoal gray suit, he looked every inch the successful, respectable lawyer, but his eyes were sending me a different message.

One side of his mouth tipped up. "Because I'm head over heels in love with the defendant," he announced.

"And because she's my wife."

The courtroom erupted. I heard a cacophony of shouting and the judge's gavel banging repeatedly, but I only had eyes for—Landon. I don't remember getting to my feet, but by the time he had walked over to our table, I was standing next to Anson Greene.

"Thanks, Counselor, I'll take it from here," Landon murmured, towering over Anson and shaking his hand. The young man's head bobbed up and down. He stuffed his papers into his briefcase and raced out of the courtroom without a word.

Landon took his place beside me. When his arm brushed against mine, an electric current shot clear down to my toes.

I looked up at him. "We're married?" I managed to croak out.

He nodded. "The ceremony at the Queen's Garden was legal." His eyes crinkled with amusement. "You really should check your e-mail more often, Kelsea."

My legs suddenly turned to spaghetti, and I collapsed into my chair. I grabbed my phone and pulled up my e-mail. There! That had to be it. *PinkLady@StJardinResort.com.*

Yoo hoo, Kelsea and Landon! (I hope you've come clean about your identity, young man. If you haven't, now would be a good time.) Imagine our shock when we were notified by the St. Jardin Historical Society about a change that went into effect on January 1. Because of new protocols outlined in the trade agreement between St. Jardin and the United States, any rituals conducted on our soil—ceremonial or otherwise—are legal and binding in both countries. The marriage ritual in which you participated is as if it took place in the US. You're legally married!

Now, I know you may be panicking right now, dear Kelsea, but don't you see? This is your Plan B! We know that Landon is crazy about you, and if you'll be honest with yourself, you'll admit that you feel the same way, too. Give him a chance. He'll show you, in more ways than you can count, how deeply he loves you.

I knew the moment I met both of you that you were meant to be together. Did I tell you that when we lived in Brooklyn, I had a bit of success as a matchmaker?

Ike says to come back to St. Jardin for a real honeymoon! It'll be on us! Love, Rosie

My mind floated back to the present to hear Landon addressing the judge.

"Your Honor, request a recess to confer with my client."

"Fifteen minutes, Mr. St. Clair." The gavel sounded.

Landon lifted me to my feet and propelled me through a side door into to a small conference room. The moment the door closed behind us, he dropped his briefcase and pulled me into his arms.

And kissed me the way I'd been dreaming of for almost three weeks.

Our kiss on St. Jardin was amazing, but this one was a thousand times better. He wasn't holding anything back this time, and neither was I.

When we finally came apart, he held me close and we just stood there, breathing heavily and rocking back and forth. "Mmm...you taste incredible," he murmured.

Thank you, Lord, for peppermint essential oil.

Landon kissed my forehead and moved his large, smooth hands to bracket my face. He lifted his head just enough to smile into my eyes.

"Happy Birthday, Kelsea."

"Happy Birthday...Landon." I loved saying his name. I had a feeling this was going to be the best birthday ever, the first of many together.

"I didn't think I'd see you till tonight, but since we're here now, I have a question to ask you."

My heart thudded. *He was going to propose!* I held my breath and swallowed a squeal.

"Will you... sleep with me now?" His smile filled his entire face, and his beautiful amber eyes danced.

I burst out laughing, and he joined me.

I smoothed my hands over his lapels and tried to calm my thundering heart. "Well, if we're married..."

"We absolutely are. I double-checked."

"Then, of course," I whispered, and he kissed me again. I looked deeply into his eyes. "I love you, Landon," I said for the first time. I whispered his name as I trailed kisses along his jawline, his cheeks, even the bump on his nose and the cleft in his chin. "I love your name. You never seemed like a Brandon to me."

He locked his hands behind my back, and I slid mine up to his broad shoulders. He looked at me sheepishly. "Well, just don't ever slip and call me that, especially around my family."

Understanding dawned. "You mean—? Your brother?"

"Yeah." He laughed and shook his head. "I don't know what got into me when I came up with that."

"I'm very glad that you're Landon," I murmured.

"So am I." His lips devoured mine in a kiss that completely curled my toes. Then he took a step back and gazed at me, his expression solemn. "I will never, ever lie to you again. Not outright, or by omission, for any reason. You have my word on that. I love you to the bottom of my soul, Kelsea."

I couldn't even speak, I was so overcome. I nodded.

His eyes searched mine. "Do you want a wedding? A real one? You never got a wedding. We could do it next fall."

He remembered. I swallowed past the lump in my throat. "You'd go through that again? You'd stand up in front of five hundred guests for me?"

He didn't hesitate. "I'd stand up in front of five *thousand* guests for you. Because I know without a doubt that you would come through that door. You wouldn't leave me standing at the altar."

Rose was right. That's how much he loves me. I swallowed. "You're right. I absolutely would come through that door. But I don't want another wedding, Landon. The one at the Queen's Garden was perfect, and it's all I want. You're all I want."

"In that case, I have another question for you," he said, his gaze steady.

Without breaking eye contact, he dropped to one knee. I wanted to memorize this moment forever.

"Kelsea Denise St. Clair." He smiled, and my soul sang at the sound of my new name. "Will you stay married to me?"

I can't resist. "We'll fight, you know. I'm full of sass."

"We will." He squeezed my hands. "And then we'll make up." His voice had gone husky.

My heart exploded with joy. "Yes, yes, yes! Of course I'll stay married to you."

Just when I thought things couldn't get any better, he stood, reached into his pocket and pulled out my tri-gold wedding band, along with a stunning diamond solitaire. "Oh, Landon," I breathed. He lifted my hand, slipped the rings on, and kissed them.

His gorgeous amber eyes melted into mine. "With this ring, I thee wed," he whispered.

I had noticed in the courtroom that he wore his ring. I kissed it and whispered the same timeless, sacred words.

Landon pulled me close. "Now, Mrs. St. Clair, we're going to go back in that courtroom, and you're going to watch your husband mop the floor with the plaintiff."

Mrs. St. Clair. My husband. I might die from happiness. "Can I afford you?" I giggled.

"Probably not, but we'll think of a way that you can pay me," he said in a completely sexy way. *Oh, my.*

As I lifted my lips for another delicious kiss, a loud rap came at the door, and we sprang apart like two teenagers caught necking.

The bailiff stuck his head in. "Time's up."

Landon picked up his briefcase and flashed me a devastating smile. "To be continued. Let's get this over with so we can start the honeymoon."

38

IF LANDON DIDN'T see for himself that the soles of his shoes were hitting the floor, he would have sworn that he was walking on air. All the doubts about his and Kelsea's relationship were settled. *She loves me and wants to be my wife!* He felt like he could take off and fly around the courtroom.

Landon was completely in his element, and the stars had aligned. He shuddered to think what might have happened had Olivia Busch not gone into labor. Sean was a good lawyer, and he would be here right now pleading Ryan's case. But he wouldn't have had any of the information that Landon was about to reveal, and with Kelsea's fate in the hands of the bumbling public defender, the case would likely have gone Ryan's way.

Landon never would have known, until after the fact, that his own firm had represented the man who had already broken Kelsea's heart and was on a self-serving mission to inflict more pain. She would have been completely devastated, and who knows if she even would have come to meet Landon tonight?

Despite all that, Sean and Olivia's situation weighed heavily on Landon's heart. He sat down next to Kelsea at the defendant's table, took her hand, and leaned in to whisper, "Say a prayer for my colleague, Sean. He's at the hospital with his wife. She's in premature labor. I'll tell you more, later."

"Of course," Kelsea whispered back, and gave his hand a squeeze.

"All rise," the bailiff announced. "Call to order the Court of the City of St. Louis. The Honorable Lawrence D. Williamson presiding."

Judge Williamson sat down and put on his glasses. "Hello again, everyone. First order of business." He looked in the direction of the plaintiff's table. "Mr. Singer, it appears that you are without counsel. If you wish to retain another firm, we will grant a seventy-two-hour continuance for you to make arrangements."

Ryan stood and cleared his throat. "Not necessary, Your Honor." He threw a smug smile toward the defendant's table and puffed out his skinny chest. "I will be representing myself."

Landon slid a glance at Kelsea and fought the laughter that bubbled in his throat. Among the many things he admired about Abraham Lincoln was his assertion that *he who represents himself has a fool for a client.*

Judge Williamson shook his head and mumbled something to himself. Maybe he was thinking of Lincoln, too. "All right then, Mr. Singer. Please proceed with your opening statement."

Landon stood. "Your Honor, I'd like to move for a dismissal."

Jasmine Singer shot to her feet. "Dismissal? Are you crazy?" she shouted.

Judge Williamson banged the gavel sharply and pointed it in her direction. "One more outburst from you, Mrs. Singer, and I will have you removed from my courtroom! Is that clear?"

The woman's face flushed bright red, and her lips settled into an angry line as she plopped down into her seat.

Landon continued. "The plaintiff is suing my client for the engagement ring or its estimated value in cash. Ms. Anderson asserts that Mr. Singer told her the ring was hers to keep. So it's a case of 'he said, she said.'"

Landon strolled to the front of the courtroom, one hand in his pocket, and turned to face the gallery. "Mr. Singer has also requested that my client remit to him one half of the value of all the deposits that were lost when he canceled their wedding and reception, in the amount of $8,400. He claims that he and Ms. Anderson wanted a very small, simple wedding, but once his mother graciously offered to pay for everything, Ms. Anderson began expanding the scope of the event, contacted vendors directly without Mrs. Singer's knowledge, and drove up the costs."

Landon looked at Kelsea, and a look of disbelief washed over her face. He knew that this was the first she was hearing any of this, and did everything in his power to send her a message.

Trust me.

He continued, "Ms. Anderson maintains that she had nothing whatsoever to do with making the arrangements, that they were completely made and paid for by Mrs. Singer."

Landon shifted his gaze to Jasmine Singer and waited for her reaction. She crossed her arms in front of her and speared him with a hateful look, but kept quiet.

Landon walked back to his table and picked up a folder. "May I approach, Your Honor?"

Judge Williamson nodded. "Yes, Counselor."

Landon went through the bar and strode confidently to the bench. "We have signed statements from eight vendors that Jasmine Singer contracted with for various services to be provided for the wedding and reception. All of them are willing to testify that they did business only with Mrs. Singer, and not one of them ever had any contact, by phone, e-mail, or in person, with Ms. Anderson. Copies of the original orders, placed by Mrs. Singer, are also provided. In every case, the original amounts contracted for were never amended."

Landon clasped his hands behind his back and waited for the judge to look over the papers. Thanks to Sean's meticulous preparation, all the vendors' names and contact information had been listed, with the intent of bolstering Ryan's claims. All Landon's paralegal team had to do was call them this afternoon, and the truth quickly came out.

Judge Williamson took off his reading glasses and set them down. "What about the plaintiff's claim that the decision to cancel the wedding was mutual, and that there was no alienation of affection on his part?"

Landon handed another folder to the judge. "We have sworn affidavits from three of Mr. Singer's co-workers. In summary, they state that he was a notorious flirt in the office, and one of them is willing to testify that two weeks before Thanksgiving, she discovered Mr. Singer and a co-worker,

Ms. Jenna Harmon, in a, shall we say, compromising position in a storeroom. We are also prepared to compel Ms. Harmon to appear as a witness to confirm documented posts on social media that she and Mr. Singer had a brief affair in late November, approximately one month before Mr. Singer and Ms. Anderson's engagement was called off."

Singer's face went white, and he jumped in his seat when his mother cuffed his shoulder from behind.

Landon had purposefully left out any reference to the pregnancy. That would be the ace in his sleeve if they ended up calling Jenna as a witness.

He couldn't stop thanking the fates that he'd trusted his instincts that first night on St. Jardin, when he'd looked on Ryan's social media page and asked his investigator to check into Jenna Harmon. With that information, his paralegal team had been able to quickly obtain the affidavits just this afternoon. Landon was already planning to give each of them a nice bonus.

Judge Williamson closed the folder and handed all the materials back to Landon. "I don't think there's any question that this is a frivolous lawsuit," he growled. "Mr. Singer, you're lucky that I'm still in the holiday spirit, and I'm not going to fine you for providing false information to your attorney. But if I ever see you in my courtroom again, all bets are off. Case dismissed." The gavel banged.

Judge Williamson stepped down from the bench, his robe billowing behind him. When he reached the door, he turned and raised his hand. "Mr. St. Clair?" he called out.

"Yes, Judge?"

"Congratulations to you and your bride."

39

LANDON CAME RIGHT to me and pulled me into his arms, and I looped my arms around his neck. "You were amazing!" I exclaimed. My heart skittered as his hands came around my waist.

"Larry Williamson is a fair judge. This may not be the most challenging case I've ever tried, but this victory is definitely the sweetest." His gorgeous amber eyes glittered and he pulled me a little closer. "Are you ready to get out of here, Mrs. St. Clair?"

"Definitely." I gave him a quick kiss, then stepped out of the circle of his arms and gathered my purse and coat while he packed his briefcase. He glanced over at the plaintiff's table and then back at me.

Landon lowered his voice. "Unless you want to wait until they're gone."

I looked around him. Ryan was slumped at the table with his head in his hands. His mother stood over him. I couldn't hear what she was saying, but it was obvious that she was spitting angry words at him.

"No way," I said with determination. "In fact, don't you need to tell Ryan when to expect your bill? That way, he can be on the lookout for it," I said innocently.

He grinned. "Remind me to stay off your bad side."

I took his arm, then switched to the other side. I looped my left hand through his elbow and wiggled my fingers. "This way they'll see my rings," I whispered.

Landon laughed softly and winked, and we set off. When we stopped in the aisle, Ryan looked up miserably, and Jasmine Singer glowered at me.

"I'll send you a bill," Landon announced. "It will include both my billable hours and Sean Busch's. Mine are at partner rate, of course. And you'll be responsible all court costs." He turned to me. "Ready to go, sweetheart?"

"More than ready, darling," I replied, and without a backward glance, I sailed back down the aisle of the courtroom on the arm of my hero, my Prince Charming, my husband.

The solid, wooden door of the courtroom closed behind us, completely shutting down that chapter of my life. I can't wait to see what God has in store for Landon and me.

He pulled me into a jubilant hug and smiled down at me. "You know what their problem is?"

I shook my head. "No, what?"

"They didn't have a Plan B."

EPILOGUE

THREE YEARS LATER

EVERY NEW YEAR'S Day, Landon and I send up an extra prayer of thanks that we both escaped what surely would have been disastrous marriages. About a year after Ryan's ridiculous case was dismissed, I heard through the grapevine that a DNA test proved that he was indeed the father of Jenna's son. I don't think either of them was ready to be a parent, and occasionally I send up a prayer for that little boy. And just a few months after that, we read in the society pages of the St. Louis *Post-Dispatch* that Nicola had married Giovanni Mancini, who had just been named manager at one of her father's luxury car dealerships.

After Landon's victory in court, we began a honeymoon that started at the Ritz Carlton and finished back on St. Jardin, where we participated once again in the ceremony at the Queen's Garden. It was the most romantic week of my life.

I asked Rose once if she and Ike knew about the change in legal status *before* the first ceremony—the one they kept insisting was just *a ritual,* and she acted as if she hadn't heard me, and changed the subject.

January is always a big month for Landon and me. The 2nd is the anniversary of the day we met, and the 8th is the anniversary of our wedding at the Queen's Garden. We always celebrate the anniversary of our engagement on the 28th, along with our birthdays. Not many couples can say that they were married for almost three weeks before they got engaged.

We go back to St. Jardin every year for our anniversary, and Rose and Ike are just the same—more in love every year, just like Landon and I are. We hope and pray for a marriage as long and as happy as theirs. Their friendship has become so very precious to us, and they're just like family.

But this year, there are two reasons that we can't go to St. Jardin, and that's okay. They're nestled together in their cradle in our bedroom. Rose Elizabeth and Isaac Anderson St. Clair arrived on January 4. Rose has my dark hair, and Isaac is a perfect little replica of Landon, right down to the cleft in his chin. Their photo and birth announcement will be in tomorrow's mail to the resort, where we've been assured a prime spot on the lobby bulletin board is ready and waiting.

Morgan, my mom, and Landon's parents have already been here and gone, and are the proudest grandparents and aunt on the planet.

Rose and Ike are coming in May to meet their namesakes, after any danger of snow and ice is long gone. After all those years of living in Brooklyn, they avoid winter at all costs. Our families are coming, too, and we're going to have the babies dedicated when everyone is here, at the little community church where Landon and I are members. I can't wait.

I heard the front door open, and my husband, the love of

my life, the father of my children, met me in the front hallway. He grows more handsome with each passing year. There are still times when I can't believe that he's all mine.

"Hi! Are they awake?"

"Hi! Happy Birthday, Kelsea," I mocked. "I'm so glad I asked you to marry me three years ago today." I tried to peek around him to see what he was hiding. "If those are roses, you *might* be off the hook."

"I'm sorry," Landon said with an endearing grin. "I just love them so much. But I love you more." He produced a huge bouquet of gorgeous red and white roses, my favorites, and my heart melted at the sight of his smile.

"Thank you," I said, breathing in their delectable scent. "They're beautiful."

He laid them on the hall table and took me into his arms. I still have a long way to go to regain my flat stomach, but it was wonderful to be able to stand toe-to-toe with him again and pull one another close. "They're nowhere near as beautiful as you. Happy Birthday, my love." His gaze drifted downward and he nuzzled my neck. "Thirty-three looks amazing on you, babe."

I took his face in my hands. "Landon," I said, trying not to laugh, "It won't look so amazing in a few months. They'll deflate once I stop nursing the babies."

His eyes sparkled. "I'll still adore you," he whispered.

I sighed dreamily, running my hands over his broad shoulders and into the hair at the base of his neck. "Just for the record, thirty-four looks absolutely incredible on you. Happy Birthday, Landon." Then he treated me to one of his magic, toe-curling kisses, and I forgot about everything else for a few moments.

"Come here." Landon took my hand and led me into the living room. "I have another gift for you," he said. "And you probably need to be sitting down for it."

I couldn't imagine. I sat down on the sofa, and Landon lowered himself down next to me. He grinned, reached into his inside pocket, and laid a key in my hand. *A house key!*

"The house? We got the house?" I squealed. "Oh, Landon!" We had put in an offer just after the babies were born on a large, beautiful home about two miles from our present one, which we were rapidly outgrowing. It wasn't the Victorian, but sometimes, you have to go with your Plan B. And sometimes, it ends up being better.

"No, we didn't get the house. Not that one, anyway."

My heart plummeted, and I looked at him in confusion. "I don't understand."

"What would be better?"

There could only be one thing. I couldn't believe it. "The Victorian?" He nodded, and I squealed and threw myself into his arms. He knew that was the home of my heart. My mind was short-circuiting. "Landon, how? I can't—you—it wasn't even for sale!" I couldn't believe it. He'd bought me my dream house?

He laughed. "It *was* for sale, for the right price. Happy Birthday, my love. Happy engagement, happy anniversary, and happy arrival of our babies." I pulled his head down for a happy kiss.

I couldn't believe it! *The Victorian* would be our home. Landon and I would raise our children there, and Mike and Maggie would be our neighbors. "It all worked out," I bubbled. "My Plan A house went away, and then we found Plan B, and then you turned Plan A into Plan B. Or would that be Plan C? Plan B went away, and you turned Plan C back into Plan A, I think."

"Huh?" Landon's eyebrows knit together. He really should be used to this by now. "Kelsea, just kiss me."

And so I did.

ABOUT THE AUTHOR

Writing is like breathing to Erin. Stories are running through her mind during most of her waking hours, and by the time she sits down at the computer, the words flow and time ceases to exist.

Erin was raised in Illinois and has lived in many places in the U.S., including on both coasts, but is a Midwest girl at heart. She spent many years as an educator from pre-school through college levels, and currently works in training and internal communications for a major global corporation.

When she's not writing, Erin loves spending time with her children and grandchildren, and playing in the garden (which equates to mostly pulling weeds) at her central Iowa home. Her secret indulgence is plain M&Ms.

Connect with Erin!
Email: ESQwrites@gmail.com
Website: www.ESQwrites.com
Facebook: Erin Stevenson Quint
Twitter: @ESQwrites

COMING SOON

Book Two in the
St. Clair Family Series

HOME TO YOU

Brandon St. Clair is one of Minneapolis' top orthopedic surgeons. Still crushed by his wife's sudden death almost a year ago, he's struggling to care for their two young daughters and find the will to keep going. Their one wish is something Brandon can't fulfill, and it breaks his heart.

Morgan Anderson is a highly respected art therapist in Chicago. Her work gives her great fulfillment, but her personal life is lonely and lacking. A deep personal secret has kept Morgan from succeeding in any long-term relationship, and she's ready to give up.

Brandon's brother is married to Morgan's sister, and they meet at a family event. Their initial dislike of one another plus the fact that they live in different states almost guarantees that they'll never connect. But sometimes God-- with a little help from a pink-haired matchmaker named Rosie--can make what seems impossible, possible.

See the next page for a sneak peek of *Home to You,* Book 2 in the St. Clair Family Series. Available November 1, 2018 on Amazon, Barnes & Noble, and eBooks.

HOME TO YOU

1

"DADDY, SHELBIE DROPPED her sippy!"

If April hadn't announced it so clearly, Shelbie's ear-piercing scream would have alerted Brandon St. Clair that something had gone very wrong in the back seat. He tried to make eye contact with his daughters in the rearview mirror, but could only see their shadowy outlines in the darkness.

"April, honey, we're almost to Uncle Landon's," he said. "Can you—" then he stopped himself. *You were about to ask a 4-year-old to climb out of her car seat to get her sister's sippy cup off the floor, while you're whizzing along the interstate at 65 miles an hour? What kind of lousy dad are you?*

Brandon switched the windshield wipers to *high* as the rain pelted down even harder. He could barely see, and it was pitch black. He consulted his phone in its dash holder, guiding him to his brother's house in suburban St. Louis. Thank God, they would be there in sixteen minutes. It was almost midnight.

He had fully intended to be there long before now, but everything that could go wrong at the hospital had gone wrong today. He'd had to cover for another doctor, and the surgical schedule was backed up. So much for Fridays being a lighter day.

By the time he'd picked up the girls from the sitter's, gotten them fed (with yet another fast-food meal), and arrived home to pack for the trip, they were already well behind schedule. Then Brandon realized he hadn't put the last load of the girls' laundry into the dryer last night, so he had to make a decision: delay their start by another hour, or take the damp clothes with them?

A trash bag filled with damp clothes rested next to their suitcases in the back.

A flash of lightning and simultaneous crash of thunder shook the vehicle, and Brandon tightened his grip on the wheel while easing his foot from the gas.

"Daddy, I'm scared!" April cried.

"I want Mommy!" Shelbie screamed.

I want Mommy, too, Brandon thought as he blinked back tears. *Oh God, why, why did you take her?*

2

MORGAN ANDERSON RESTED her chin on her hand and gazed at her sister. "Motherhood totally suits you," she said with a smile.

Kelsea St. Clair lifted her sleeping daughter up to her shoulder and rubbed her back. "It's the most exhausting thing I've ever been through, but I love every minute of it."

Her husband, Landon, entered the room. "I'm not so sure we love it at three in the morning," he quipped, with an affectionate squeeze of his wife's shoulder. He held out his arms. "You want me to take her?"

"Sure, thanks," Kelsea replied, and Morgan watched as they made the seamless transfer. She tried to ignore the way that her sister and Landon operated as one mind, one heart. Morgan swallowed, and turned her attention back to the baby.

"She's really out," she commented. Little Rose hadn't made a peep.

Kelsea yawned and looked up at her husband. "How's Isaac?"

"Fine. Hopefully he'll sleep a few hours before he needs to eat again."

Morgan was so proud of her sister. "You're really brave, nursing twins. But it's the best thing for them. Good for you."

Kelsea looked at Landon. "Have you heard from Brandon?"

"Yeah, they should be here in about fifteen minutes." He left the room with the baby.

Morgan glanced at her phone. "Oh, gosh, is it that late already?" She'd lost track of the time, as was usually the case when she and Kelsea got together. Morgan had driven down from Chicago and thankfully arrived before the spring storm.

She had never met Landon's brother, but knew about the tragic car accident that had taken his wife early last summer. "You know, it's kind of weird that I've never met Brandon," Morgan mused. "You and Landon have been together over three years now, and I've spent some holidays with you."

Kelsea put her chin in her hand. "Well, we really haven't seen him that much, either. When Darla was still alive, one of them was always on call, or she was pregnant with one of the girls or had just given birth, or something."

"So, what's the schedule for the weekend?" Morgan asked. "Or have you figured that out yet?" She stifled a laugh.

Kelsea feigned indignance. "Hey, I'm getting better! But I don't have a printed itinerary like you would," she teased. They both laughed. Kelsea was famous for flying by the seat of her pants. Morgan and their mom were the planners in the family.

"Mom will arrive sometime tomorrow afternoon," Kelsea said. "Landon and Brandon's parents will be here sometime then, too. We'll all go to the Spaghetti Factory for dinner tomorrow night, and then church on Sunday, and a barbeque back here."

"Don't forget the babies' dedication service," Morgan said.

"Of course! The whole reason you're all here," Kelsea said with a smile. "I *love* the outfits you got them to wear. They're just precious."

"Well, they're the most beautiful babies in the world, and I'm the proudest aunt ever!" Morgan had discovered that she absolutely loved shopping for baby clothes.

Kelsea reached over and squeezed Morgan's hand. "Thank you." Her expression turned serious. "Be honest with me. Does it bother you at all—you know—"

"What? To see you being a mother? Kels, no! Not at all. I'm so happy for you and Landon. I adore the babies, and *love* being an aunt." Kelsea had been her rock when Morgan discovered that she would probably never be able to have children.

Silence settled itself over the two sisters like a warm blanket, and Morgan's heart began to quicken. *I guess this is as good a time as any.* "Kels, I, um—I need to tell you something." She took a deep breath. "I—oh wow, this harder than I thought it would be."

Worry settled over her sister's dark brown eyes. "Morgy, what's wrong? Are you sick again? Are you—"

Morgan shook her head adamantly. "Oh, no—I'm fine. I didn't mean to scare you. It's just—" she took another breath. "I've been thinking about maybe adopting a baby."

Kelsea's jaw dropped, and her eyes grew large. She grabbed Morgan's hand. "Oh, Morgy, that's fantastic!" Her eyes teared up.

"Yeah, well—" Morgan gave a nervous little laugh and tucked a strand of hair behind her ear. "It's such a big step, but I'm not getting any younger, and I'll probably never get married, and even if I do, I still can't—well, you know."

Kelsea squeezed her hand. "You don't know that, Morgan," she said softly. "But what got you thinking about this?"

Morgan wiped a wayward tear from her eye. "Well, you know I've been working with that arts program with preschoolers in the inner city," she said. Kelsea nodded. "There are so many children who need a loving home. A lot of the children in the program are orphans, and it just got me thinking. You and I are both big advocates for adoption." One of their best friends from high school was adopted, and they both knew other families who had adopted children.

Morgan shrugged. "Anyway, you know me and my planning." The two sisters laughed together. "So just pray for me, that God will make His will clear on this. It's a huge decision."

"I sure will," Kelsea said warmly.

Morgan chewed her lower lip. "And keep it to yourself for now, okay?"

"Of course."

"Now, back to this weekend," Morgan said, closing the door on that subject. "When do the guests of honor arrive? I can't wait to meet them."

Kelsea's eyes lit up. "Rosie and Ike's flight gets in at eleven-thirty tomorrow morning. I can't wait to see them. It's been more than a year." Rose and Ike Goldman owned a resort on a Caribbean island where Landon and Kelsea had met, and had become like family to the young couple. "I hope you're okay staying at Maggie and Mike's with them," she added, referring to hers and Landon's best friends who lived across the street.

"Of course," Morgan said. "They have plenty of room for all of us, and I'll be there to help Rosie and Ike if they need it."

"Maggie practically begged me to house some of you there! I wanted you here, but Landon thought it would be better for his brother and the girls to be close to us." She looked at Morgan apologetically.

Morgan reached out and touched her sister's hand. "Kels, you don't need to apologize. I know it's a difficult situation. How's he doing, anyway?"

Kelsea shook her head. "Not great. He's super-doctor-in-control at work, and a hot mess otherwise."

"Does he have any help with the girls, other than daycare?"

"No, he's determined to handle the home front on his own. And he's still so broken and lost without Darla. I think Landon and their parents are going to try to talk with him this weekend."

"Well, I should probably get back to Mike & Maggie's," Morgan said. "They gave me the front door code and said to stay here as long as I wanted to." She stood, and Kelsea got to her feet and held her arms out. The two sisters hugged.

"I'm so glad you're here, Morgy," Kelsea whispered.

Morgan snorted softly and pulled back. "You know you're the only one who's allowed to call me that, don't you?" She looked into her sister's dark brown eyes and smiled.

"Yes, and you're the only one who can call me Sissy," Kelsea replied with a smile.

A bright bolt of lightning flashed outside, illuminating the living room window, and the women held their breath, bracing themselves. Still, they both jumped when a crack of thunder boomed a mere second later.

And then, the lights flickered out.

"Gosh, that's close!" Morgan exclaimed, her hand on her chest.

Landon's voice called out, "Honey, don't move. I'm coming with flashlights." The sisters huddled together until he arrived.

"Are Penny and Sheldon okay?" Kelsea's Pomeranians had been a big part of her life even before she met Landon.

He came into the room. "They're fine. They're completely zonked out on our bed."

Kelsea looked at Morgan. "Maybe you should stay here," Landon held out a flashlight.

"I'll be fine. It's just across the street," Morgan replied. She put her hand up. "Guys, I'll be fine."

Kelsea walked with her to the front door, and opened it. "Oh, wow, it's pouring!" She quickly reached into the hall closet. "Here, at least take this," she said, and handed Morgan a big umbrella.

"Thanks, I think I'll need it." She squeezed Kelsea's hand. "Love you, see you tomorrow."

"Yes, come for pancakes around nine. Oh! Would you babysit so Landon and I can go to the airport?"

You can do this. "I'd love to!" Morgan grinned.

"Thanks! Sleep well, Morgy."

3

BRANDON COULDN'T THINK of anything but getting off the road and out of the rain. He was so tired, and he had a headache. That last crack of thunder ushered in a chorus of wailing from his young daughters, which only added to the pounding in his head. The lightning must have hit a transformer, because all the lights around them went out.

He'd turned his phone off because it was almost dead. *LaBonne Terrace,* that's what he was looking for. Had Landon told him it was the first house on the left, or the right, after the road curved? Brandon came to an intersection and slowed to try to read the sign. He couldn't really see it, but it looked like it might start with an *L,* so he turned right. He knew he was probably going a little too fast, but there were no other cars on the road, and he just wanted to get there.

"Big Victorian house with a circular driveway," he repeated his brother's instructions to himself. Brandon looked left, hardly able to see anything in the downpour.

As he looked right, a sudden movement flashed in the headlights, and he instinctively slammed on his brakes. Was it an animal? Brandon's mouth dropped open and his heart leapt into his throat. He clutched the steering wheel as his heart pounded in his ears.

An indistinguishable figure, hunched under an umbrella, dashed across the road just in front of the SUV.

I almost hit someone. The idiot just ran out in front of me, didn't even look! The realization sent white-hot anger racing through his veins. Without thinking, he rolled down his window.

"Hey!" He screamed. "What is WRONG with you?"

The figure slowed, but didn't stop, and the person's head was almost totally obscured by the umbrella. He was medium height, but that's all Brandon could make out.

"Where do you think you are, the Indianapolis Speedway?" a woman's voice shouted.

I almost hit a woman.

www.ingramcontent.com/pod-product-compliance
Lightning Source LLC
Chambersburg PA
CBHW030246130626
46549CB00002B/415